OMETHEUS PROJECT: TRAPPED

"A fun and fantastic read." —The Super Mom

"My class loved it. They were totally engaged. It's a hard book to put down."

—Jeff Montag, 5th Grade Teacher
As Quoted in the *San Diego Union-Tribune*

"Keeps you turning the pages. It had me hooked by page two of the first book."   —The Children's Book Review

"An entertaining novel . . . that reads in a flash."
—Bookloons Reviews

"The gripping storyline will make young readers read this story in one sitting and want a sequel. I strongly recommend this book."   —The Midwest Book Review

"I did not want to stop reading."
—8th Grade Student
Published in the Newsletter of the ISTA

"Fun and suspenseful. Highly recommended."
—Kirkus Discoveries

"Brings to mind the classic young reader's novel *A Wrinkle in Time*. An adventure story for young and old alike."
—Associated Content

"Brilliant science adventure stories—perfect for a class reader for 9-13s, and a 'must' for any school library. These books are, I hope, the first of a long series!"

—*Primary Science* (UK)

"Nonstop action adventure ... You really can't put the book down for very long. A thrilling read."

—California Science Teachers Association

"Would make a great read-aloud and would foster much talk among families."   —*The Old Schoolhouse Magazine*

"A suspenseful thriller that you will not want to put down. . . . vividly written."   —*The Science Reflector*

"If you have a middle schooler that is into science or sci-fi, buy this book. If you have a reluctant reader who has an interest in science or adventure stories, buy this book."

—Amateur de Livre

"I read this book with my class for the first time this year and my class loved it."

—President, Idaho Science Teachers Association

Praise for
THE PROMETHEUS PROJECT: CAPTURED

"A page turner that kids—and their parents—will love reading . . . thrilling adventure."
—Catherine Hughes, Sr. Editor
National Geographic KIDS magazine

"Fast paced adventure, mixed with quick thinking. Ryan and Regan are great fun, and the story is just a cool idea! Very well written."   —TeensReadToo.com (5 stars)

"I would give this book three-thumbs-up, but I only have two thumbs."
—7th grader, published in the Newsletter of the MSTA

"Fast paced and full of action."   —*ForeWord Magazine*

"I was captivated by *Captured*. I found the second book in this great series as entertaining and action filled as the first book."   —TCM Reviews

"An intense storyline that will have you churning through the book without putting it down."   —The Super Mom

"A sequel that matches the pace and excitement of the original. In *Captured,* the author has added a second gem to the reading treasure chest."   —The Reading Tub

"A delightful tale of kids working together, much as you would find in the *Lemony Snicket* books. Readers will look forward to more."

—Curled Up With a Good Kids Book

"Will keep you on the edge of your seat while begging you to read on . . . full of fast paced action (that) keeps the reader wanting more. I eagerly await the third book."

—Steve Fielman, Director-at-large,
Intermediate Science, New York State

"Holds even an adult readers attention to the very end. I look forward to his next offering in the series."

—AAAS

"With *Captured,* the author continues to tell a story that leaves the reader reaching for chapter after chapter with plenty of suspense and cliff hangers. This is a fun and adventurous story."

—California Science Teachers Association

The Prometheus Project

Book 1

Trapped

The Prometheus Project

Book 1
Trapped

Douglas E. Richards

Paragon Press

Copyright © 2004 by Douglas E. Richards
Paragon Press edition copyright © 2010

Second Edition Published by Paragon Press, 2010
ParagonPressSF@gmail.com

ISBN: 978-0-9826184-1-7

Library of Congress Control Number: 2009944189

Printed in the United States of America

First Paragon Edition

Contents

Chapter 1   Top Secret 3

Chapter 2   Razor-Wire and Laser Beams 9

Chapter 3   Shot on Sight? 17

Chapter 4   Guards and Radiation 23

Chapter 5   Breaking the Code 31

Chapter 6   Two Minutes From Capture 37

Chapter 7   Captured 41

Chapter 8   The World's Biggest Secret 47

Chapter 9   Big Trouble 53

Chapter 10   Playing With Fire 59

Chapter 11   Spider Webs and Diamonds 65

Chapter 12   Secrets and Peril 71

Chapter 13   Bug Attack! 77

Chapter 14   Vanishing Act 83

Chapter 15   Trapped! 87

Chapter 16   Technology and Magic 97

CONTENTS

Chapter 17   The Unearthly Zoo 101
Chapter 18   Predator 105
Chapter 19   The Swarm 113
Chapter 20   Repairs 121
Chapter 21   The Universe-Wide-Web 127
Chapter 22   The Answer 139
Chapter 23   A Race Against Time 149
Chapter 24   History Repeats Itself 153
Chapter 25   Seeing Double 157
Chapter 26   The Challenge of Prometheus 163
Chapter 27   Part of the Team 171

The Prometheus Project

Book 1

Trapped

CHAPTER 1

Top-Secret

Ryan Resnick sat on the floor of the attic and examined the contents of yet another cardboard storage box in the dim attic light—a magnifying glass, a pair of high-powered binoculars, an old phone and various picnic supplies. He shook his head and frowned.

Beside him his sister, Regan, two years younger, was also searching through boxes without success. She had shoulder-length strawberry blond hair, a freckled face, and green eyes that almost always sparkled happily—or at least they had until six weeks before. "Are you *sure* it's up here?" she asked her brother for the second time.

"*Yes*. Mom had the movers put the boxes with sporting equipment up here until she and Dad could sort it out. Keep looking."

Frisbee Golf was a good idea, he thought, but it was a lot harder to play *without* the Frisbee. He had used it last in San Diego. Back when he had a life. Back when he relished every new day instead of dreading it. Back six weeks before—an eternity ago.

It was still hard to believe that their lives had been ruined so quickly. And without any warning. Just six weeks earlier school was out, the summer was just beginning, and everything was great. Great, that is, until the day they were told they would be moving three thousand miles away from California to a nowhere place in the middle of the woods called Brewster, Pennsylvania. More like *Snooze-ter,* Pennsylvania.

Their parents, both scientists, had decided to leave the university to work at a company named Proact. One minute the Resnick kids were excitedly awaiting a summer filled with friends and fun and the next they were in the middle of a little town with no friends—or even other *kids* for that matter—and nothing to do all day except climb trees and watch grass grow. And perhaps play Frisbee Golf—if they could ever find the blasted Frisbee.

How could their parents do this to them! Was it possible to die of boredom? It was clear that they were going to find out.

A faint voice from below Ryan startled him from his thoughts.

"Where are the kids?"

It was their father! He must have just entered his upstairs office, just below where they were sitting in the attic.

"I called before we left Prometheus Alpha," answered

the equally faint voice of their mother. "They said they were going to find a good spot to create a Frisbee golf course and play. They said they'd be back in an hour or so." Their mom sighed so heavily they could hear it even through the floor of the attic. "They didn't sound good. They're still mad at us. I can't say I blame them."

"I know this move has been rough on them. But they'll adjust. Really. They just need a little time. And you know we didn't have a choice."

"But *they* don't know that. I can't stand lying to them. If only we could tell them the truth about why we're here, I'm sure they would understand." There was a long pause. "At least my mother will be back in a few days so they won't have to be home alone anymore."

In the attic, the kids had not missed a word of the conversation, staying still as statues and barely breathing. Their grandmother had been staying with them for most of the summer but had left that morning for a three-day trip. Ryan had convinced his mother—barely—that he and his sister could look out for themselves during the day while their grandmother was away. Their parents could go to work as usual. He and Regan were very responsible, he argued. Besides, what kind of trouble could they get into here in Snooze-ter, Pennsylvania anyway—forget to look both ways while crossing the woods and get hit by a speeding tree?

But the part about being home alone wasn't the part of their parents' conversation they were thinking about at the moment. *Their mom and dad were lying to them!* Why? What were their parents *really* doing here? What was Prometheus Alpha? Why didn't they have a choice about moving here? *What in the world was going on?*

They were still digesting these startling revelations as their father continued. "We can't tell them the truth. You know that. If we did, we could all find ourselves in a prison somewhere. And if they told others, the consequences could be far worse even than that—far worse." He paused and then added gently, "You know I don't like it any more than you do."

There was a long silence in the room. Finally, their father made an obvious attempt to change the subject. "Have you checked the monitors yet?"

Their mother sighed loudly once again. "Yes," she said. "No indication of electronic bugs or directional listening devices of any kind. We're secure."

Regan's eyes grew wide. Was she dreaming all of this? Was she in a bad spy movie? She glanced at Ryan and raised her eyebrows questioningly.

Ryan put a finger to his lips. When he first heard his parents he had planned on descending from the attic to reveal they were home, but not now. He felt guilty spying on them like this, but something weird was going on and he needed to learn more about it. *They could all end up in a prison somewhere? What were his parents involved with?*

"Good," said their father. "We can head back to Prometheus in a few minutes."

"Why did they kick us out now of all times?" said their mother in obvious frustration. "On the day that we finally broke in."

"Exactly because *it is* the day we finally broke in. Months ahead of schedule. Security was caught off-guard. Instead of months to implement massive upgrades they now have days. We won't be the only ones working around the clock from now on."

"Don't you think we're covered already? They put in an invisible state-of-the-art laser alarm system and the only entrance to Prometheus is protected by a building that could withstand a nuclear strike. How much more do we need?"

"Apparently a lot more. Now that we've broken in the security chief thinks the current setup is an embarrassment. It won't be long before they install fingerprint scans, retina scans, voice-print scans—you name it, they'll be scanning it. Right now security is beginning the installation of video cameras that will monitor the entire perimeter as a supplement to the lasers. Even though it won't be completed for a few days they had to shut off the laser alarm system for a few minutes to install some cable. Even during this short shutdown policy dictates that all non-security personnel be evacuated. The good news is that they've decided to take care of another security matter while everyone is gone so they won't have to ask us to leave again."

"What security matter is that?"

"A software upgrade. They'll also do a comprehensive scan of all computer systems and a full reset of all passwords."

"I suppose then we need to decide on new passwords before we go back. Any ideas?" asked Mrs. Resnick.

"As a matter of fact, yes," answered their father. "I think you'll like these. Here, let me write them out for you."

There was silence for several long moments before Mrs. Resnick spoke again. "I like the elevator password. *We are in the middle of nowhere.* Very cleverly done. But why did you choose this particular number as the door password?"

"It's in alphabetical order."

There was a long pause. "I see what you did. Very clever."

"You didn't know you married such a clever guy, huh."

"Well, I guess your success at pulling off the most difficult break-in in history to get to the greatest treasure of all time might just qualify as clever," she teased. "And," she added wryly, "you even managed to do it without getting us all killed."

"Very true," he responded playfully. And then, after a long pause and a heavy sigh, he added grimly, "At least not yet."

CHAPTER 2

Razor-Wire and Laser Beams

Ryan and Regan waited for five minutes after their parents left the house—just to be sure—and climbed down from the attic to the second floor hallway in silence.

"What was that all about?" said Regan.

Ryan shook his head. *Good question.* His green eyes reflected worry and his short, light-brown hair was in disarray from having run his hand through his hair as he tried to make sense of what he had heard. The high-powered binoculars he had found in the attic were now hanging from a strap around his neck. "I wish I knew," he said in frustration. "Mom and Dad are involved in something shady. And dangerous." He held up the binoculars. "I think we need to learn more about Proact," he said decisively.

Not waiting for a response, Ryan walked into his

father's office with his sister following and carefully removed a dictionary from the shelf. He quickly flipped through it. "Prometheus," he mumbled as he turned pages. "Prometheus. Prometheus. Here it is," he said at last. He cleared his throat. "Prometheus," he read aloud. "A Titan of Greek mythology who stole fire from the Gods and gave it to mankind as a gift." *Stole fire,* thought Ryan. *So Prometheus was a thief. Just great.* He frowned deeply and looked up to see his sister grinning from ear to ear.

"Why are you smiling?" he asked her.

"I was just picturing Prometheus trying to gift-wrap fire. You know *that* couldn't have been easy."

Ryan laughed, but his smile quickly faded as he returned to the problem at hand. "So Mom and Dad are involved in something very secret called the Prometheus Project," he said in a serious tone. "And Prometheus turns out to be a thief." He closed the dictionary and placed it back on the shelf. "Dad did mention a treasure and 'breaking in' somewhere. I can't believe Mom and Dad would be involved in something criminal, though."

Regan nodded. "Me either."

"Somehow, we have to figure out what's going on."

They discussed the events of the past six weeks to see if this could help them answer any questions raised by their parents' conversation. It didn't. All it accomplished was to raise *additional* questions to add to the puzzle.

Something had been fishy about the move from the beginning. Their parents were top scientists who frequently received job offers from around the world. They had always refused because they loved their jobs at the university and were not willing to leave San Diego. Until now.

So what had changed? Why had they felt they had no other choice but to move to Pennsylvania? Why did they have to leave immediately? And why would a company locate in a place as isolated as Snooze-ter? The town was mostly woods and farmland. The roads were not even paved—just dirt or gravel. Their new house was the only one for quite a distance. Proact was hastily clearing trees and building a large housing development about a mile away—the Resnicks were scheduled to move there in three months or so—but nothing was ready now.

They had no choice but to investigate further. And that meant a trip to the Proact facility. They had never been there before but they knew it was several miles south of them along a dirt road. They jumped on their bikes and pedaled like crazy. Before long they spotted a large Proact sign off in the distance. They immediately exited the road and biked into the woods until they were out of sight. They parked by a tall tree and quickly climbed up onto some of its higher branches. Secure in the tree, they turned to get their first view of the now mysterious Proact facility.

It was surrounded by the most wicked-looking chain-link fence either of them had ever seen. A lethal, two-foot high coil of spiked wire, wound very tightly, ran along the top of the entire length of fence, like a giant steel slinky made almost entirely of knife blades. The fence created a square enclosure about a quarter of a mile on each side.

Regan shook her head, almost unable to believe her eyes. "I've seen barbed-wire fences before, but this is like something out of a horror movie. This makes regular barbed-wire look like a joke."

"Yeah," said her brother, nodding slowly. "I've heard about this stuff. I think it's called *razor-wire*."

Regan studied the fence more closely and realized that the tightly spaced blades were exactly that—razors—with pointed barbs at both ends. "It's well named," she noted grimly. Their dad had mentioned a laser alarm system and video monitors soon to come, but the sight of this deadly razor-wire barrier left no room for doubt. Their mom had been correct. This place had some *serious* security.

Off to one corner they quickly spotted the main Pro-act building. It was large, modern and very impressive. It was also unfinished. *Unfinished?* So why the hurry for their parents to come here?

Off in the distance they could see what appeared to be large signs attached to the perimeter fence at regular intervals. Ryan lifted the binoculars, put them to his eyes, and focused in on one of the signs.

WARNING—DO NOT ENTER!
INTRUDERS WILL BE SHOT ON SIGHT!

He swallowed hard. Saying nothing he handed the binoculars to his sister sitting on the branch beside him. He watched a troubled look come over her face as she read one of the signs.

"Not exactly what I would call a friendly greeting," she noted wryly.

Ryan nodded. "I guess they ran out of the signs that say, 'Welcome To Proact' with bright yellow happy faces painted on them."

Regan smiled as she continued scanning. A few seconds later she pointed and said, "Can you see those men just inside the fence over there?"

Ryan followed her finger and could make out four men near the fence, looking small in the distance. *What were they doing?*

Regan carefully turned a small dial on the front of the binoculars to improve the focus. "They must be the ones who shut down the laser alarm system. It looks to me as if they're checking to make sure it was reset properly." She paused. "Take a look."

Ryan put the binoculars to his eyes. Two of the men

were throwing powder high into the air and watching intently. The falling powder passed through two previously invisible laser beams, each the thickness of a broom handle, and in so doing turned them both red and easy to see. Ryan had seen a movie about a thief trying to steal a diamond from the middle of a room protected by countless such invisible beams crisscrossing the floor—lasers of the type that only produced light and not searing heat. Anything that blocked one of the beams for even an instant, like part of a thief's body, triggered an alarm. Particles from a powder mist, however, could make the beams temporarily visible without fully blocking them and setting off the alarms.

The beams ran parallel to the fence-line—about three feet in from it. One beam was about a foot above the ground and the other was about four feet up. Someone who managed the impossible task of getting through the fence without being cut to ribbons, and without being seen by the cameras, would still have a nasty little surprise waiting for them when they took their first step or two and walked through one or both of the invisible beams.

Ryan's brow furrowed in deep concentration.

An interesting thought occurred to him.

He used the binoculars to carefully explore the entire fence perimeter, foot by foot, looking intently for something in particular. After five minutes, he found it.

He lowered the binoculars. It was time for them to leave. They needed to beat their parents home.

But it was now crystal clear to him what he had to do the next morning, and despite the warm summer weather the thought of it brought a chill to his spine.

CHAPTER 3

Shot on Sight?

Ryan and Regan set their alarms for five thirty the next morning and awoke to find that their parents were already out of the house. Just how early had they left? When their dad had indicated they would be working around the clock he had not been kidding.

By six thirty the two kids were back in the same tree branch they had been in the day before.

"Okay," began Ryan as he looked out over the Pro-act grounds from his perch in the tree. "Mom and Dad could be spies and they could be criminals. Worse, they could be here against their will, being threatened in some way if they don't cooperate. We need to figure this out and we need to do it quickly." He saw agreement in his sister's eyes. "Do you have any theories?" he asked her.

She paused in thought for a few seconds and then shook her head no.

Ryan frowned. "Yeah, me neither. And I have a bad feeling that we're not going to get anywhere by sitting here in this tree, talking about it, and guessing what might be happening. We need more information."

Regan raised her eyebrows. She could tell her brother had come up with a plan. "What do you have in mind?" she asked.

Ryan took a deep breath and then said, "I think we need to get inside the Proact building and snoop around. See what we can learn. I think it's our only chance to get to the bottom of this." He paused to let his words sink in. "But if we're going to do it, we need to do it now. I mean like *today*."

"I don't get it. Why such a big hurry?"

"Because they're about to finish putting in all the video cameras."

"Ryan, it's not like they need the *cameras* to keep us out," she said, rolling her eyes. She nodded toward the fence. "Even if we could get through the million-razor-blades-of-death over there—which is totally impossible—the laser alarm system is still working."

The corners of Ryan's mouth curled up into just a hint of a smile. "Who said anything about getting *through* the fence?" he said. Without another word he handed his sister the binoculars and pointed to the east. "Take a look."

She put the binoculars to her eyes and followed his finger. "What am I looking for?"

"The woods are pretty thick around here so there are hundreds of trees near the fence. But one of the trees has a branch that's grown over the razor-wire. Do you see what I'm talking about?"

About thirty seconds later Regan nodded. *Very interesting.* The branch ended only a few feet inside the fence line, but it was enough. They could easily crawl along it to get beyond the fat coil of razor-wire. *Very, very interesting.* "What about the laser alarm system?"

"Not such a problem if you know it exists and you know exactly where it is. Luckily, I do." He pulled two plastic bags filled with a white powder out of his pants pocket. "I filled a couple of sandwich bags before we left with talcum powder. All I have to do is make the beams visible with this."

Regan nodded. He had thought things through quite carefully. Once the beams were visible they *would* be fairly easy to avoid. "Great plan," she said admiringly. "Well, we won't be bored today, that's for sure."

Ryan nodded. "I'm glad you're okay with the idea. I was a bit worried you might not be. So you stay in the tree near the fence with the binoculars as a lookout while I check out Proact. Hopefully, I won't be gone more than an hour or so."

"What! What are you talking about?" She shook her head adamantly. "I'm not waiting for you in a tree. Even if I saw something I couldn't warn you anyway. I'm coming with you."

"I can't let you do that Regs," said Ryan protectively. "It's too dangerous. Remember all the 'intruders will be shot on sight' signs?"

"How could I forget. But they won't shoot a couple of kids."

"Are you positive about that?"

"Positive. They just put the signs up to scare people so they won't trespass," insisted Regan.

"Well then, I guess it's a good thing for them they didn't use the 'Welcome to Proact' signs with bright yellow smiley faces after all. Probably not as scary."

"Probably not," agreed Regan, grinning. She quickly turned serious once again. "If we were large men carrying guns they probably *would* shoot on sight. But we're just a couple of kids. They'll even be less nervous if *I'm* with you. I'm younger than you and pretty short for my age. Since we won't look threatening, they'll want to catch us first and ask us questions—you know, *before* they shoot us."

"Thanks, that's very comforting," said Ryan, rolling his eyes. He shook his head. "But you still aren't coming."

Despite his last words, Regan knew she was beginning to convince him. "Come on Ryan. You *need* me. They won't hurt a small, harmless girl. And we're in this thing together. Besides," she added with finality, "you don't have a choice. I'm coming whether you want me to or not."

He sighed heavily. He really couldn't stop her if she

insisted on going with him, and he had seen the determined look she now wore on her face many times before. He had learned from experience that once she set her mind to something, no power on Earth could get her to change it. "All right," he said finally. "You're in."

He was impressed. He and Regan fought a lot but he had to admit she was sharp and gutsy. Now she was showing him that she had even more guts than he had thought. He had worried it would be tough to convince her to let him go on this insane mission, and instead she had convinced him to let *her* come along. And he realized to his surprise that he was very glad she had.

"Let's do it," said Ryan as he rose from his perch in the tree. "I do have to admit that we won't be bored today. *Dead* maybe," he added wryly as he began his climb down to the ground. "But definitely not bored."

CHAPTER 4

Guards and Radiation

Thirty minutes later Ryan was clinging to the tree limb that extended over the fence. They had agreed if they got caught he would do the talking while Regan would look small and innocent. He would explain they had been on their bikes, had seen the tree limb running over the fence, and decided to use it as a short-cut to visit their parents. They would play dumb if asked about anything else.

Ryan searched long and hard for any guards. All was clear. He slid along the branch until he made it over the fence. He was now ten or eleven feet off the ground and more than a little stressed. The branch hadn't seemed all that high when he was looking up, but now that he was looking down and preparing to jump, the ground seemed awfully far away. He took a deep breath and lowered himself the full length of his body. He searched for the flattest, softest landing site possible and prepared to let go.

And froze!

A man inside the fence had appeared from nowhere and was coming straight toward him! Worse still, the man had a gun, and it was drawn! Ryan's heart beat like a jackhammer in his chest. He quickly pulled his legs up under him so they weren't dangling down at the man's eye level.

The man hadn't looked up yet, but he would in a matter of seconds. And even if he didn't, Ryan couldn't hold on for much longer! They would be caught before they had even begun. He was a sitting—or in this case, hanging—duck.

"Jim, come in!" bellowed an anxious voice from the man's waist. "Emergency! Jim, do you read?"

The man holstered his gun and lifted a small walkie-talkie from his belt, bringing it to his mouth. "Collins here," he said quickly.

"Jim, we've got a problem," squawked the walkie-talkie. "Make your way to the west perimeter immediately! We spotted two intruders . . ." There was a long hesitation. "Coming *out* of Prometheus Alpha."

The walkie-talkie almost slipped from the man's grasp and he had to juggle it before he regained his hold. "Did you say *out*?" he said in astonishment. "That's *impossible*. No intruders have ever gotten *in*," he insisted.

"Well apparently *these* two did," snapped the voice. "And Jim," he continued. "We think they're kids."

The man—Jim—looked at the walkie-talkie in disbelief. *"Kids?"*

"We think so. Alan almost had them but they made it to the west woods. I want you to join him in the search," the other man ordered. "Immediately. We have to find them!"

Ryan listened as he fought to hold on, very near the limit of his endurance. His muscles were aching and he was certain his arms would pop out of their sockets at any moment.

Just as his hands finally slipped from around the branch the man turned and began racing off at a full sprint in the other direction. Ryan landed as quietly as possible and held his breath. They were safe! At least for now.

Ryan froze in a crouch for several minutes until the man was out of sight and then motioned to his sister. Moments later she joined him on the ground. He would never tell her so, but he was impressed. The height from which he had dropped had seemed awfully scary, yet Regan—because she was smaller —had plunged an even greater distance, and without hesitation. He didn't know any other girl her age who would have had the nerve to do the same.

"Did you hear that guy mention Prometheus?" whispered Ryan.

"Yeah," his sister whispered back. "I wonder who those kids are that they're after."

Ryan scratched his head. "I don't have any idea. I guess just a few kids who wandered into the wrong place at the wrong time. Lucky for me they did, or that guard would have caught me for sure." He breathed a sigh of relief as he reflected on just how helpless he had been hanging from a tree, a mere ten feet from both an "intruders will be shot on sight" sign and a heavily armed guard moving steadily toward him.

Ryan pulled the bag of talcum powder from his pocket once again. He scooped out a handful of the fine, white powder and tossed it out in front of him. As expected, two bright red laser beams magically became visible where they sliced through the billowing white cloud that he had created. Lowering his head and right shoulder, Ryan carefully threw his body forward, hands extended, and rolled between the two beams onto his shoulder, making sure to lift his legs high enough to easily clear the lower beam. Regan repeated this maneuver and quickly joined him on the other side of the hidden laser perimeter.

So far, so good.

Crouching low, they headed toward the main building, alert for security guards. They chose an indirect path to their destination, avoiding being out in the open at all costs, staying in the cover of trees and high weeds. Soon they passed a bunker-like gray building constructed of huge slabs of thick concrete. It was about the size of a very large house, and almost entirely hidden by trees and thick growth. There were no windows or openings of any kind to mar the plain, ugly, rectangular structure, except for a huge steel door, so big it encompassed almost an entire side of the building. A large metal sign hung above the door.

DANGER!
RADIOACTIVE WASTE STORAGE.
LETHAL RADIATION LEVELS INSIDE.
DO NOT ENTER!

Ryan shook his head. What was with this place? Every sign warned of impending death. Why couldn't the sign have said, *Free Chocolate Inside*?

Ryan began moving toward the Proact building again when his sister touched his arm. She pointed at the concrete building. "I think we should go in there and check it out."

"Go in *there*?" repeated Ryan as if he had heard wrong. "I don't think so. The lethal radiation in there isn't going to wait before harming us because you're little and cute."

"You really think I'm cute?" said Regan, smiling.

"No, of course not," insisted Ryan, trying to cover for having accidentally done the unthinkable, giving his sister a compliment. "You know that wasn't my point."

"Let's think about this for a second, Ryan. The Pro-act building isn't finished yet and it's totally out in the open. This building *is* finished and also well hidden. You wouldn't see it unless you almost walked into it like we did. Then, to top it off, they put a giant radiation warning sign on it. They *really, really* don't want people to enter this building, which means they're hiding something important inside. The sign is just a fake to scare people away."

"And what if there really is deadly radiation inside? What if you're wrong?"

She thought for a moment and then smiled. "If I'm wrong, then I guess we'll be the only kids in Pennsylvania who will glow in the dark."

Ryan smiled despite himself. She had certainly made some good points. But even if the radiation warning was a bluff, it was too big a risk to take. As much as the little brat could drive him crazy, he was the older brother. It was still his job to protect her. It had been his idea to break onto the grounds and he had endangered her enough just letting her come with him. No, he would not be the one responsible for her getting hurt. "There's no way we're going inside," he said firmly, but then after a brief pause added, "but I guess it can't hurt to take a closer look."

Regan nodded. At least it was a step in the right direction, and she could make another attempt to convince him later.

They carefully approached the large steel door. The steel looked to be just as thick as the concrete, but there was no door handle or knob of any kind. Why have a warning sign when there was no way to enter anyway? As far as they could tell, the building was completely sealed. Ryan stepped closer to touch the door. He reached out with his right hand and—

Ryan jumped back as if he had been shocked! When he touched the door a panel near his hand had slid open to reveal a steel keypad, with numbers zero through nine. It had startled him nearly to death.

"Please enter a ten-digit password," said a computer voice from a small speaker at the bottom of the keypad. *"Please note that an alarm will sound immediately if an incorrect digit is entered."*

Regan raised her eyebrows. "Radioactive waste storage facility, huh?" she said. "Very interesting, don't you think?"

Ryan nodded. "You were right," he said, now convinced. "Something very important must be going on inside this building." He took a determined step closer to the door. "Let's find out what it is."

Chapter 5

Breaking the Code

"I'm glad we now agree that we need to get inside," said Regan. "Now all we have to do is find a way to, ah . . . get inside."

Ryan ignored her attempted humor. His expression was one of total concentration. "I'll bet the numeric password we heard Mom and Dad talk about will do the trick."

"You may be right. But we never actually heard what it was."

"No, but we should be able to figure it out from Dad's clue."

Regan considered. Her brother was right. Their dad loved riddles and brainteasers and word puzzles, and since they were old enough to talk he was always challenging them to solve a wide variety of them. "Dad said the number is in alphabetical order," she offered.

"Right. So what does that mean?"

"0-1-2-3-4-5-6-7-8-9?"

Ryan shook his head. "Can't be. Mom wouldn't have needed Dad's help to make sense of a number *that* obvious. Besides, that's in numerical order. He said alphabetical."

"True. But the keypad only has numbers on it, not letters. How can you put *numbers* in alphabetical order?"

Ryan scratched his head. *Good question.* "What if you spelled out each of the numbers zero through nine," he said, thinking aloud. *Could it really be that easy?* "Regan," he said excitedly. "Recite the alphabet for me very slowly."

Regan didn't hesitate. Maybe Ryan was on to something. "A."

Ryan mumbled the numbers zero through nine to himself, deep in concentration. He nodded for her to continue. "B," she said. Regan made it to the letter E before her brother stopped her.

"Okay," he said. "Now we're getting somewhere. None of the numbers zero through nine begin with A,B,C or D. But Eight starts with an E. I'm betting this is the first digit. The problem is we can't make even a single mistake. What do you think?"

Regan was pleased that he had asked for her opinion. "I think we should risk it."

Ryan nodded. "Here goes nothing."

Mentally bracing himself for the earsplitting sound of an alarm, which would be followed quickly by heavily armed guards, he reached out and pushed the 8 button on the key-pad. Regan cringed beside him as she waited to see—or hear—the outcome.

Nothing happened. No sirens, no blaring alarms.

"Fantastic!" said Regan. "You did it. Let's keep going. F," she recited excitedly.

Her brother mumbled to himself again as he counted. When he reached Four he nodded and reached out for the keypad. His finger found the number 4 and pushed . . .

"Stop!" shouted Regan beside him.

He had been an instant away from pressing the button and was just able to jerk his hand away in time. *"What?"* he snapped. "What is it?"

Regan raised her eyebrows. "Five," she said simply.

"Five?" he repeated, and then her meaning began to register. His eyes went wide. Whoops. She was right! He had nearly been too hasty and blown it. F-O-U-R and F-I-V-E both began with F, but Five came before Four alphabetically.

Ryan made sure there were no other F numbers in the digits zero through nine and then pressed the 5 button followed by the 4. Again, they heard nothing but the welcome sound of silence. "Nice work, Regs," he said appreciatively. She had saved them.

Regan beamed and continued reciting the alphabet. After a short time they had entered 8-5-4-9-1-7-6-3 and 2. Nine digits. The number 0 would complete the password, the first digit numerically and the last alphabetically.

Ryan took a deep breath and reached toward the keypad one last time. He pushed the 0 key and quickly stepped back. What would happen?

An electric motor whirred as the giant door separated in the middle and the two sections slid smoothly apart.

They were in!

Ryan inched his way toward the opening in the door and cautiously peered inside the building. Other than a shiny, all steel structure at its center, it was completely empty. No rooms. No people. No equipment. And thankfully, no containers of radioactive waste.

They entered the building and inspected it carefully. It soon became clear that the rectangular steel structure Ryan had seen was an elevator, about the size of a large, three-car garage, but with a ceiling three times as high. It was by far the largest elevator they had ever seen. Was the entire purpose of the building to house and protect this elevator?

As they approached to within a foot of the elevator its massive doors slid open with barely a sound. They traded a quick glance and then carefully stepped inside. The doors slid shut behind them.

The elevator was empty except for a computer monitor that was set inside one of its walls and a metal keyboard that was attached to the wall underneath it. There were only two elevator buttons, labeled *up* and *down*, next to the keyboard.

Regan reached out toward the *down* button and looked back at her brother questioningly. He nodded. She took a deep breath and pushed. Where would the elevator lead?

A loud *thunk* came from the elevator doors, startling them. It sounded like a bank vault closing. *"Warning,"* said a computer voice from a speaker in the ceiling. *"You have attempted to activate the elevator without first keying in your twelve-letter password. The elevator doors have now been sealed. You have two minutes to enter a correct password or security will be alerted.*

"Repeat. You have two minutes to enter a correct password or security will be alerted."

Chapter 6

Two Minutes From Capture

Regan rushed to the door and tried to pry it open. Not surprisingly, it wouldn't budge. She banged angrily on the door with the sides of her fists. "We're trapped!" she yelled anxiously. They were in big trouble now.

Ryan fought to remain calm. "We still have two minutes," he said quickly. "Let's not panic. We can get out of this. Mom and Dad said that one of the new passwords they created was for an elevator. I'm betting it was for *this* elevator. Do you remember?"

"That's right! Mom said the password was **'We are in the middle of nowhere'**. Good going, Ryan! Quick, let's punch it in."

Ryan shook his head. "The computer asked for a twelve-letter password, remember?"

"How many letters are there in 'we are in the middle of nowhere'?"

"Too many. Let's find out exactly. Count them while I start spelling." He recited each letter in the phrase hastily and looked expectantly at Regan for a letter count.

"Twenty-five" she said, frowning. "You're right. Far too many. As crazy as it seems, this must be the password for a different elevator."

"I don't think so. How many password protected elevators can there be? This has to be the right password. Somehow. There must be a trick to it. Dad wrote it down for Mom. If there wasn't a trick to it he could have just told her what it was."

"Right," said Regan, encouraged. "And when Mom saw it she told him he was clever."

Ryan rubbed his hand through his hair as if to stimulate his brain. "Is there any way to write this sentence using only twelve letters?"

Regan considered the question carefully. "Maybe there is!" she said, her eyes growing wide. "Last year Dad challenged me to write 'I see you are a cutie' using only seven letters."

Ryan thought about this for only a second before he saw the answer. "I . . . C . . . U . . . R . . . A . . . Q . . . T" he said. Regan was on to something here. "Typical Dad puzzle. People do this sort of thing on their car's license plates to shorten messages. I bet this is what Dad did with the password."

"You have . . . sixty seconds . . . to enter a correct password," announced the computer.

Regan refused to let the annoying computer voice distract her or to think about the seconds that were quickly ticking away. "Okay, let me give it a try. You count this time," she said and without waiting began to work on shrinking the password. "WE. R. N. T. MID-L. OF. NO—"

"Still too many!" interrupted Ryan hurriedly. "And that's using N for 'in' and T for 'the', which I don't think Dad would do. Too sloppy."

"You have . . . thirty seconds . . . to enter a correct password."

"There *have to be* other tricks for shortening a message. What are we missing!" challenged Regan frantically.

Ryan continued to think furiously. She was right. There had to be another trick. But what was it? He held his head in his hands and tried to block everything else out.

"You have . . . fifteen seconds . . . to enter a correct password. Fourteen, Thirteen, Twelve—"

Regan felt sick to her stomach. If they had been caught outside they could have acted like innocent kids just looking for their parents to say hello. Now it would be obvious they weren't innocent. Now there was no way they could just play dumb. She braced herself as the computer counted down the last few seconds remaining.

Ryan's head shot up from his hands and his eyes widened as inspiration hit him full force. He had it! The password. At least he thought he did. If only he could enter it in time. His fingers raced over the metal keyboard as the computer continued its countdown to disaster. Regan looked on in astonishment.

"—Three, Two, One—"

Ryan stabbed at the last key as the computer calmly spoke what had suddenly become a horrifying word.

"Zero."

CHAPTER 7

Captured

The elevator was totally silent now that the count-down had stopped. Ryan was sure he had been too late. He imagined dozens of guards racing to the elevator.

Time seemed to stop. A second ticked by.

"Correct password entered," said the computer. *"Security procedures have been aborted. Repeat, security procedures have been aborted."*

"You did it Ryan!" screamed Regan happily. She gave her brother a puzzled look. "But how? What did you enter?"

Ryan smiled. "I remembered another trick to making short words stand for longer phrases—where and how the words are written. Dad and I had lunch at a restaurant about a year ago while you and Mom were at a birthday party and he jotted down some riddles for me to solve while we waited for our food. He wrote the word "Headache" with each letter split in half and told me it was a shortcut to say something longer. The answer was 'splitting headache'. Do you get it?"

Regan thought about it for a moment and then, smiling, she nodded.

"Another one he did was 'b e d'. The answer was 'bedspread'—the word 'bed' *spread* out. But my favorite was 'HOrobOD'. Robin Hood. The word 'Rob' in the word 'Hood'. ROB in HOOD. Once I remembered this lunch, and knowing Dad, it was easy to solve the password. If you stick the words **we are** in the middle of the word **NOWHERE,** you have **NO-we-are-WHERE,**" he explained. "**We are**" in the middle of "**NOWHERE.**"

Regan had counted as he spelled the password. N-O-w-e -a-r-e-W-H-E-R-E. Twelve letters exactly. "Nice going!" she said. "And you figured it out in *plenty* of time," she teased. "You had an entire half-second to spare."

Ryan laughed. "Better late than never."

As much as he wanted to celebrate this victory for a while longer he knew that they were running out of time and they still hadn't learned what was happening here and how their parents fit in. He put his finger on the down button. "Ready?"

Regan nodded. "Let's see where this thing goes," she said far more bravely than she felt.

Ryan pushed the button and the elevator began a rapid descent. In just a few moments they would be at their destination, probably a basement facility ten or twenty feet down, hopefully a giant step closer to solving the mystery of Proact.

Ten seconds passed. Then twenty. Then forty-five. The elevator continued to pick up speed as it dropped them deeper and deeper into the earth. It was now falling at a considerable speed. They looked at each other in alarm. When would it stop? How far down could they possibly be going?

After what seemed like ages the elevator halted suddenly, causing their already nervous stomachs to jump to their throats. They had arrived.

"Ah . . . Ry," said Regan thinly. "How far down do you think we are?"

"I don't know," he answered grimly. "But at least the length of a good-sized skyscraper, maybe two."

She gulped as the doors opened slowly. They peered out cautiously.

They were in a huge cavern, roughly spherical, about the size of a large baseball stadium. A cavern with an expansive, thirty foot ceiling. The air was damp and cool and powerful electric lights attached to the walls illuminated the area.

They stepped from the elevator onto the rock floor before them, their eyes wide. There was machinery and high-tech equipment everywhere. Scores of heavy, treaded vehicles were parked along one wall, some resembling bulldozers and others military tanks with ten-foot-wide drill-bits where the turrets should have been. An impressive display of machinery. But no people. The cavern was as deserted as a ghost town. It was also perfectly symmetrical and smooth. It was clearly not a natural cave. Incredible! Excavating a cavern of this size so far beneath the surface must have been an enormous job. Why had it been done?

All thoughts of how the cave was created were swept from their minds instantly by what they saw against the far wall. What in the world?

They walked toward it almost as if in a trance. Dozens of high-powered, high-temperature lasers were unleashing a fury of lava-red beams toward the wall. The beams were evenly spaced so that they created a perfect rectangle of blazing, continuous energy against it. And lasers were only the beginning. Arrays of generators and other equipment of unknown purpose were pointed at the wall, also, contributing what was certain to be massive levels of invisible forces and energies.

Inside the rectangle formed by the blazing lasers the wall shimmered in an ever-changing rainbow of colors. How could this wall—or anything for that matter— withstand this awesome onslaught of heat and energy?

"Amazing," whispered Regan.

"What do you suppose—"

Regan shrieked as two men popped through the shimmering, rectangular kaleidoscope of colors outlined by the beams, from behind it. Like ghosts walking through a wall.

Their reaction to Regan's scream was immediate. Rolling in opposite directions, they each came up on one knee. They were so expert in this maneuver that the guns they were now pointing at the two young intruders had appeared in their hands as if by magic.

"Freeze!" shouted the man to their right. "Make one move and it'll be your last!" he finished menacingly.

CHAPTER 8

The World's Biggest Secret

Paralyzed with fear, the Resnick siblings couldn't have moved if they wanted to.

"Dan! What are you doing?" barked the man on their left to the man who had threatened them. "They're only kids. You're going to scare them to death."

He turned toward the petrified kids. His features softened and he lowered his gun. "Ah . . . sorry," he offered. "My name is Carl. My partner Dan here got a little carried away." Like his partner, he was tall, trim and carried himself with confidence and athletic ease. Without question both of these men had been elite members of the military at one time. "You surprised the living daylights out of us just now and I guess our training took over," finished Carl apologetically.

Ryan's temporarily frozen heart started beating again. "That's okay," he whispered hoarsely, barely finding his voice. "You surprised us, too." He paused. "Anyway, we, ah . . . we were just leaving, so we'll, ah . . . we'll just be on our way."

Carl smiled and shook his head. "Good try," he said, walking over to his partner and standing beside him. "I think you know you're going to have to come with us. You have a lot of explaining to do. It should have been *impossible* for you to get down here," he said in disbelief. "And you're in some world-class trouble." He gently pushed his partner's arm down so his gun was no longer pointing at them. "But I can assure you that no one is going to shoot you."

"Let's go," ordered Dan gruffly, leading them away from the rectangle the laser beam perimeter had created—now clearly a doorway of some kind. Their eyes still told them that the shimmering, multicolored doorway formed a solid barrier. But it wasn't solid at all. The men had come from the other side—and had walked through completely unharmed. And without question, on the other side of this doorway was the secret they had come to learn.

Regan refused to let this chance slip away. Carl had said he wouldn't shoot them. They were already in huge trouble. What did they have to lose? "H . . . h . . . hold on a second," she croaked. "I don't feel so hot." She put one hand to her head and one to her stomach, wincing in pain. She bent at the waist, holding her hips. "That elevator ride and those . . . swirling colors . . . making me . . . dizzy . . . and queasy . . . and—"

She stumbled two or three steps forward, toward the doorway, and fell to her knees. She put her head in her hands and made a series of loud, heaving, throaty sounds as if everything she had ever eaten in her entire life was now erupting from her mouth like lava from a volcano. Her retching sounds echoed throughout the cavern.

Ryan ran forward and stooped down beside her. "Regan, are you okay?" he asked worriedly. She caught his eye and gave him a quick wink. She then shifted her eyes suggestively toward the doorway before quickly returning them to her brother.

Ryan caught her meaning instantly. She was good, he thought in admiration. Very good. He nodded ever so slightly to let her know he understood and was in. He was game if she was.

Ryan glanced up at the guards as his sister continued her performance. The two men had backed up a few steps and had turned away, looking somewhat ill themselves as they listened in disgust to what they thought was Regan heaving her guts out onto the floor.

"Now!" shouted Regan as she sprang up and dived through the multicolored doorway with Ryan close behind, taking the guards completely by surprise. As they hit the doorway they felt an electric tingle—the same

and-needles sensation as if their foot or arm had
been asleep, except that they felt it *everywhere*—for
just an instant. And then they were through.

They were through! They had actually made it!

Their mouths fell open in shock. They were outside!

Outside?

Impossible. They were still thousands of feet underground.

But underground or not, the place they were in
stretched on as far as they could see in every direction,
including straight up.

But they weren't really outside either. There was no
sky! Just open space stretching as far up as the eye could
see. No sun. No blue. No clouds of any kind.

It was as if they were in a well-lighted building so
vast that they couldn't see any of the walls or ceiling.
But how could any light source other than the sun illu-
minate such a huge space? And the light wasn't coming
from any one place. It was *everywhere*.

The air was fresh and clean, like outside country air
would be, not damp and chilly like the air in the cavern
had been.

The landscape was dotted with exotic buildings of
every kind and flowers and vegetation unlike anything
they had ever seen before. To their left was a structure
that was the size of a house but perfectly spherical, with
a mirrored surface that reflected its surroundings in daz-
zling brilliance. Just beside this globe was a transparent

building that seemed to be suspended in midair. Another building was morphing from one fantastic geometric shape to another continuously before their eyes.

They were so spellbound by the sight of this astonishing place that they completely forgot the trouble they were in. Regan was rudely brought back to reality by a firm grip on her arm. "Feeling better now!" snapped Dan angrily.

Regan gulped. "Much better, thanks," she croaked.

"What is this place?" asked Ryan in wonder.

Carl sighed. "You are standing in a city built by an alien race using technology thousands of years more advanced than ours. A city that also happens to be the biggest secret on Earth. And now you kids know about it!"

Regan swallowed hard. "So what does that mean exactly?" she asked timidly.

"It means," said Carl angrily, "that you kids are in trouble. Big, big trouble."

CHAPTER 9

Big Trouble

"Follow me," ordered Carl.

He stepped on what was clearly designed as a sidewalk or walking path. Ryan and Regan followed and Dan took up the rear.

The surface of the walking path was extraordinary. It was soft and cushiony and at the exact right moment it would trampoline them forward so that their steps were effortless. Ryan guessed it was allowing them to walk three or four times faster than usual. "It almost seems as if this walkway is alive," he whispered in wonder. "As if it's intelligent and knows exactly when to bounce us so we don't ever lose our balance."

"I know what you mean," agreed Carl. "In fact, this entire city almost seems alive to me sometimes."

"Ah . . . where are we going?" asked Regan, not sure she wanted to know.

"A building about a twenty minute walk from here—well, twenty minutes as long as we stay on this walkway. This is the only walking path we've found so far and it leads directly to the entrance of a single building, so we decided this building was worth investigating."

"So what's all this about?" asked Ryan. "How did you find this city? Do aliens live here? Do you—"

"Save your questions," interrupted Carl. "Until we arrive."

Twenty minutes later, after passing a cluster of domed buildings, they spotted their destination, a five story building in the shape of a soccer ball made from a light blue, metallic material.

Sure enough, the path led right up to the entrance of the building and stopped there. Soon they had entered and made their way toward a massive oval doorway that served as the entrance to an even more massive room. The entrance was cluttered with heavy equipment including several blowtorches and electrical generators. Inside, fifteen or twenty people in white lab coats were all gathered around an airy staircase made of thread. The thread formed net stairs so thin they were nearly invisible. Three other scientists were sitting on individual stairs and looked almost as if they were floating, yet somehow the stairs supported their weight. The scientists had affixed a thick pole firmly to the staircase and a spotlight, an electrical generator, and several other heavy pieces of equipment had been bolted to the pole.

A man was on his knees, carefully placing a small piece of the staircase webbing in a container with a pair of tweezers. The others looked on in celebration, cheering and patting each other on the back.

Several scientists turned as they approached. Two of them were particularly familiar.

"Mom! Dad!" shouted the kids in excitement, rushing forward into the arms of their thunderstruck parents.

Their mom, Amanda Resnick, was a short, attractive woman with soft features, blue eyes, and strawberry blonde hair like Regan's, although cut shorter. Now, however, she looked sick to her stomach and wore an expression of shock, horror, dismay and worry all at the same time. "Are you alright?" she asked anxiously.

Ryan nodded while Regan found herself speechless.

Benjamin Resnick was a short man with a friendly face who always looked a little sloppy. His shirt never managed to stay tucked in and his brown hair was always pointing in several directions. Now, however, his eyes gleamed with demon-like intensity. "Regan, how about you?"

Regan looked up at her father. The man in front of her was no longer the frumpy, playful, teddy-bear daddy she had long known. Instead, at that moment, her father had transformed into a man Regan was certain would take on the entire world singlehandedly if anyone or anything had hurt his children.

"We're okay Dad," she assured him. "Really."

Mr. Resnick studied his two children carefully for several seconds to satisfy himself that they really were, in fact, okay, before finally turning to Carl. "What's all this about?" he demanded.

Carl met his stare. "I blew it, Ben," he said simply. "I can't tell you how sorry I am about this. Your kids defeated our security. It's as simple as that."

"Defeated security?" repeated Amanda Resnick in dismay. "You can't be serious. Are you telling me that these kids made it past a razor-wire fence, the laser perimeter, *and* your guards patrolling outside?"

"No," said Carl miserably. "I'm telling you that they did all that, *and then* came up with correct passwords to get into Prometheus Alpha. *And then* tricked me to get into this city after they were caught."

An older scientist stepped forward. He was white-haired and grandfatherly, with a pear-shaped body, a beard, and inch-thick glasses. "How did they manage to do all this, Carl?" he asked.

Carl shook his head. "I don't know, Harry. Given that they're Ben and Amanda's kids, I thought it best to bring them here immediately rather than interrogate them."

The white-haired scientist nodded. "Ryan, Regan, could you tell us how you happened to end up here today."

Both kids swallowed hard. They were surprised to be addressed by name, but both realized they shouldn't be. While they didn't know any of the scientists in the room their parents obviously did.

"Go ahead kids," instructed their mom. "This is very serious, so be totally honest and don't leave anything out."

It took ten minutes for them to complete their story and answer questions.

"Thank you," said the white-haired scientist when they had finished. "I appreciate your honesty. My name is Dr. Harry Harris. As you may have guessed, I am the one in charge here. First, let me say that I'm quite impressed. You two are remarkably clever and resourceful. Your parents didn't violate any security procedures and I can't fault them for having such clever children. I can't fault you two for acting on your understandable suspicions. I can't fault Carl's security either—you beat it fairly and squarely. Unfortunately," he continued, "none of this changes the fact that we now have a big problem on our hands. We need to figure out what we're going to do now."

"We didn't mean to cause so much trouble," said Regan softly. "We just wanted to know what was going on here." She paused and scratched her head. "Come to think of it, what *is* going on here?"

"You can't blame them for being curious, Harry,"

said her mom. "Is there any reason, now, not to tell them? After all, they've made it this far."

Dr. Harris considered. She had a good point. And he wasn't against finding an excuse to put off deciding what to do about this situation for a few more minutes.

He nodded. "Go ahead and tell them."

CHAPTER 10

Playing With Fire

Amanda Resnick knew the current circumstances could not have been worse, but at least she would finally have the chance to tell her children the truth. "About one year ago," she began, "an oil prospecting company was drilling for oil in the ground above us when they began to break drills. And not little dentist drills either. They used enormous and incredibly powerful industrial oil drills that were supposed to be unstoppable. In time, they determined that there was something buried deep in the earth at this location that they just couldn't drill through, no matter what they tried.

"After several months," continued their mother, "the company finally gave up and left. But a government agency had learned of these strange events and sent a small team of experts to secretly investigate. It didn't take them long to realize they were dealing with something well beyond any human technology: a solid wall of energy unlike anything known to science. Proof that humanity is not alone in the universe! The energy barrier—or force-field if you will—was in the shape of a hollow hockey-puck; a disk about one mile around and thirty feet high." She gestured to Dr. Harris. "Harry, would you like to go on from here."

Dr. Harris nodded. "After this discovery the project was given our nation's highest top-secret classification and renamed *Prometheus,* and I was put in charge. Although the energy barrier was paper-thin, nothing we could throw at it could even scratch it. We tried flame-throwers, acid, explosives—you name it, we tried it—and got absolutely nowhere. Then, by accident, one of our attempts at least caused a section to become transparent. It didn't break the barrier but at least we could see through it. In so doing we discovered this incredible city," he said triumphantly, still obviously awestruck by the enormity of this finding.

Ryan raised his hand timidly. "Ah, sorry to interrupt," he said. "But I must have misunderstood. I thought you said the force-field enclosed a space about a mile around and thirty feet high, and that this city was inside. But surely this city is far, far bigger than that."

Dr. Harris smiled. "Indeed it is, Ryan. I'm pleased that you picked up on that. So how is this possible? We have no idea. How do you fit an elephant inside a shoebox without shrinking the elephant? Figuring out the science behind this little trick will be a top priority."

Dr. Harris paused for a moment to remember where he was in the story and then continued. "We could now see the city through the barrier, but we couldn't get to it. The greatest archeological, scientific, and technological find in history looked to be in perfect condition, and it was less than a centimeter away through the barrier. But unless we could break through, it might as well have been in another galaxy. And based on everything we knew, my people were telling me it couldn't be done." He paused. "That was when we called in your father. He was the perfect choice. He was one of only three physicists in the world we thought might at least have a *chance* of success, and we already knew we would want your mother to be part of any team we formed later."

Amanda Resnick was a top biologist who specialized in modeling how life might have evolved on different planets—alien life—and what the chemical and biological building blocks for this life might be. She had worked with NASA to look for signs of life on Mars. She would, indeed, be someone Harry Harris would seek out immediately to be part of the Prometheus Project.

Dr. Harris continued. "Your father analyzed our data and conducted several experiments on the barrier. After weeks of calculations he told us he believed if we assembled some very specialized equipment and tied it in to a high-speed computer, he might be able to create a high-energy counter-field. A field he hoped could alter the polarity of the barrier enough to punch an opening in it. He went home and immediately began working out the mathematics needed to create this counter-field. Meanwhile, we worked around the clock to carve out the cavern you visited—Prometheus Alpha. We finished the cavern six weeks ago."

Ryan nodded. Six weeks ago—an eternity. It made perfect sense now. Exactly when they had moved to Brewster.

"Your father wasn't sure he could do it," continued Dr. Harris. He looked at Ben Resnick with great respect. "But I never had a doubt. I didn't wait for him to succeed. I began gathering a team of scientists from every field to study the city. I recruited everyone here." He smiled broadly. "And your father has more than justified my confidence in him. In only six weeks he did the impossible. It was truly brilliant work."

The Resnick siblings looked at their father proudly. Most of the time they thought of their parents as just plain old Mom and Dad and forgot just how impressive they really were.

"In fact," Dr. Harris went on, "your father succeeded just yesterday, three months ahead of our most optimistic estimates. I finished recruiting and assembling all the members of the Prometheus team just in time," he added, smiling proudly. His smile quickly turned to a frown. "Then again, my recruiting duties are not exactly over. I'm only halfway finished hiring for Proact."

"I don't understand," said Ryan. "Aren't Proact and Prometheus the same thing?"

"Yes and no," replied Dr. Harris. "The name 'Proact', by the way, is a combination of 'Pro' from Prometheus and 'a.c.t.'—alien city technology'. We formed the company as a cover for our activities but also for other important purposes. The Prometheus team members will have offices and labs in the Proact building and will be officially employed there. Proact will have extensive and ultra-secure scientific facilities we can use to study what we find in the city. But most Proact scientists will not be part of Prometheus. We will recruit hundreds of scientists to work on their own advanced projects. The Prometheus team can use the scientific insights we gain from our study of this city to help these scientists further their projects—without ever telling them where these insights originated, of course. They will work in the Proact building but will never know about this city. Only the handful of people in this room will ever know the truth." Dr. Harris realized what he had just said and frowned deeply. "And you weren't supposed to be among that handful," he added pointedly.

"Have you found any aliens?" asked Regan quickly, trying to change the subject.

"Not so far. We think the city is abandoned. Why it was built and why it is empty are just two of the many mysteries of this place. But what we will learn here is sure to change the course of human history forever."

"Like the gift of fire did," noted Ryan. "That's why you named this the Prometheus Project, isn't it?"

"Exactly right," said Dr. Harris, impressed that Ryan knew about the Greek myth of Prometheus and was able to reason out the relevance of the name. "Prometheus stole fire from the Gods and gave it to mankind. This city offers us the *technology* of the Gods. But of equal importance, the name is also a reminder for us to be cautious and mature with our use of what we find here. Like fire, used incorrectly, the technology in this city could be extremely dangerous. We have insisted that our efforts here will be to advance human science for the *good* of humanity, not to make either weapons or money. The president agreed."

There was a long pause. "Any more questions?" asked Dr. Harris finally.

"By president," said Regan, "I suppose you mean . . ."

"The President of the United States, of course," said Dr. Harris matter-of-factly.

CHAPTER 11

Spider Webs and Diamonds

The President of the United States! The Resnick kids traded wide-eyed glances. Incredible!

It was then that the full impact of everything they had just been told sunk in. Of course the president. Given what they had just learned, his involvement made perfect sense. In fact, everything now made sense. Their parents' secrecy, the security here—even why their parents felt they had no choice but to finally leave San Diego to come here. You didn't turn down a chance to be a part of the most important discovery in history. And they had been angry with their parents for moving here! If they had only known.

"In fact, the president will be visiting next week," continued Harry Harris. "He wanted to come here yesterday, right after your father breached the force-field, but we asked him to wait until we've had some time to explore. We want to be sure his visit is as safe and informative as possible." He paused and adjusted his thick glasses absentmindedly. "Well, that should do it," he announced. "I believe you're now fully up to speed."

"I just have one more question," persisted Ryan. "What were you celebrating when we arrived?"

His mom gestured toward the wispy staircase. "Last night we decided to cut out some of these threads to study. It turned out to be far easier said than done. After a number of failed attempts, we finally managed it. We were celebrating our success."

"Why would it be so difficult just to cut some threads?" asked Regan.

Amanda Resnick smiled. "They're a lot stronger than they look."

"*Mom*, I know *that*," said Regan in a tone that suggested her mother had just questioned her intelligence. It was totally obvious that a collection of threads so thin as to be almost invisible, yet still able to easily support the weight of an adult, had to have some special properties. "But, I mean, just how strong are we talking about here?"

"As strong as anything we've ever seen except the force-field," replied her mom. "Far stronger even than spider silk," she added, as though this were the ultimate compliment.

"Spider silk?" repeated Ryan in disbelief. "Spider silk isn't *strong*. You can break a web with no effort at all."

Mrs. Resnick raised her eyebrows. "I don't know

Ryan, there are a lot of insects who might not agree with you," she said, an amused smile coming over her face. "Remember that each thread of a spider web is far thinner than a strand of human hair—hundreds of times thinner, in fact. And yet a web can still stop a large, flying bug. A web of equally thin threads—but made of the world's toughest steel instead of spider silk—wouldn't be *nearly* as strong. Put another way, if you could make a web out of spider-silk ropes as thick as a pencil, this web would stop a jet airplane."

"Wow," said Ryan, truly impressed. "I never thought about it that way."

"Most people don't," said his mom. She pointed to the staircase. "And these threads are *millions* of times stronger even than spider silk. We finally began to appreciate just what we were dealing with when our every attempt to cut out a piece for study failed. Our initial efforts failed to even *scratch* one of these delicate-looking threads. We finally succeeded using a specially made diamond saw, with very fine teeth."

Regan raised her eyebrows. "A diamond saw?"

"A saw with a blade made out of diamond."

"Why make a saw out of diamonds?" asked Regan, still confused.

Mrs. Resnick smiled. "Diamonds aren't just used for jewelry and decoration. They also happen to be the hardest natural material on Earth, so hard they can even scratch glass. So diamonds are used to make the best saws and drills. Luckily for us the saw worked and we were able to get a sample. The secret of these threads alone could revolutionize dozens of fields: architecture, engineering, aviation, space travel—the list goes on and on."

"And this is only the beginning of what we might learn from the wonders of this place," added their father. "The force-field. The material in the walking path that makes walking so effortless. Even the light-source for the city, which we haven't even found yet. All of this, and we've been here less than two days!"

"The technology here really is amazing," agreed Regan. "It almost seems more like magic than science," she said.

Dr. Harris smiled gently. "If you took someone from two hundred years ago and brought them to the present day, they would think that *our* technology was magic. Think about it. Television, computers, jet airplanes, electricity, cell phones. They wouldn't have any idea how these things worked. They wouldn't even know what these things *were*."

A thought struck Regan. "Wouldn't that also be dangerous for them?" she asked. "What if they stuck a finger in an electrical socket to find out what it was?"

"Excellent point," said her mom. "That's one reason we're trying to be so careful here. We never know when we're about to stick our finger in the alien equivalent of an innocent looking socket. Prometheus gave a very powerful, but very dangerous, gift to mankind."

Amanda Resnick frowned deeply. "But without question this city is the most dangerous gift humanity has ever received."

Chapter 12

Secrets and Peril

The room became eerily silent. Every scientist in the room had long since considered the dangers of tinkering with technology far beyond current human understanding, but Mrs. Resnick's statement had been a forceful reminder of this point.

Finally, Dr. Harris cleared his throat to break the tension in the room and said, "I think it's time to come back to the issue at hand. What do we do now that these kids know about the Prometheus Project?" He paused and rubbed his chin in thought. After almost a minute had passed he finally shook his head and said, "I'm afraid I don't have a ready answer." He turned toward the security chief. "Carl," he said, "you're the expert in these matters and most qualified to make this decision. I'll stand behind whatever you decide."

Carl nodded solemnly.

"It goes without saying," said Ben Resnick, his brown eyes now locked onto Carl's in a cool, unblinking gaze, "that you're not just deciding what to do about two kids, but what to do about me and Amanda as well."

Carl nodded unhappily. "Yes. I do realize that. This is truly a horrible situation with no easy answers. This does not involve criminals, spies from other nations, saboteurs or terrorists. That would be easy. No, this involves innocent kids who are the children of two of our key scientists. Not to mention that Ben here just made an incalculable contribution to this project. Yet the importance of keeping this project absolutely secret could not be greater."

"We won't tell anyone," pleaded Regan. "We swear."

Ryan vigorously nodded his agreement beside her.

Carl pursed his lips but said nothing. He considered the two young intruders in silence for an agonizingly long time, his mind obviously running through a number of possibilities. No one in the room spoke or even seemed to breathe. "Although I believe it is a great risk," he said at last, "it may very well be that trusting you to keep this absolutely secret is the best option we have."

"But kids are terrible at keeping secrets—even if their intentions are good," said a plump woman with glasses who, like most of the scientists in the room, had remained silent until this point.

The same is true of most adults, thought Carl, but aloud he said, "We don't have a choice. Not a real one, anyway."

The head of security sighed and turned toward the kids with a very serious, and very troubled, expression. "Listen very closely," he said. "I need for you to understand just what is at stake here. This city could easily change the world's balance of power. Even though we don't intend to apply what we learn here to create weapons—the world has plenty of these already—there are many governments that would never believe us. If they knew this city was in our hands they would panic. It's not a stretch to say that this panic could ultimately lead to World-War Three."

Ryan and Regan gulped.

"Are you with me so far?" said Carl.

They both nodded. Every word was etched in their minds.

"This is one possible nightmarish consequence of this secret getting out. But there are many others. What if terrorist groups got wind of this? What would they be willing to do to try to get this city under their control? The technology here could make them unstoppable." He paused. "I could go on for hours, but I trust you get the point."

"Absolutely," croaked Ryan while Regan nodded beside him.

"Good. The stakes could not be higher. Because of this we have considerable power to protect this secret. If you keep this a secret, everything will be just fine. But if we ever learn you discussed this project, or joked about it, or talked in your sleep at a campout about it, we'll be all out of pleasant options."

He turned toward Ben and Amanda Resnick and gave an apologetic look. "And your parents will be affected as well. What options am I talking about? Imprisonment. Planting evidence that your entire family has a history of mental illness leading you all to rant about aliens and spies and ray-guns. Probably both. And if you fail to keep this secret, don't think for a moment that we won't find out. We will."

Carl leaned in as he finished, looming over his far smaller listeners to add even more menace to his words. "Now—have I made myself perfectly clear?"

"Perfectly," they both whispered at the same time.

"Amanda? Ben?"

"Understood," said Mr. Resnick. "Given the circumstances, this is a very fair solution. I know my kids. They will keep this a secret."

"Kids," said Dr. Harris gently. "I can't tell you how sorry I am that this has happened and how sorry I am that the seriousness of this situation had to be spelled out in this way. If we could undo things so you would never discover this city we would. We have truly placed a great and terrible responsibility on your young shoulders." He nodded solemnly at them. "But given the initiative, guts, and cleverness you displayed finding your way here, I'm confident that you're up to it."

"We won't let you down, Dr. Harris," Ryan assured him. He took a deep breath and mustered his courage. "Now that this is settled . . ." he began. "Now that this is settled . . . can we . . . well, can we help you explore this city?"

Dr. Harris shook his head as if he had heard wrong. "What?" The entire group looked just as shocked. "Are you *kidding*?"

"Ah . . . no," said Ryan timidly. Then, far more firmly added, "Why not? It's a huge city and you have a very small team. We would stay out of your way and I know that we could help."

"Ryan's right," added Regan. "We *could* help. You could think of us as assistants. We could do whatever you told us to do."

"We promise not to cause any trouble," insisted Ryan.

"I'm afraid it's totally out of the question," said Dr. Harris. "You heard your mother. This city is likely to be the most dangerous place on Earth."

"I don't know, Harry," said a tall, bald-headed scientist. "Maybe the kids have a point. We could use all the help we can get. And we're being extremely careful to limit the danger. I know it would be unusual, but I think adding a couple of bright kids to the team could prove very valuable. I think they could turn out to make unexpected contributions. Kids aren't afraid to think of ideas that adults would consider crazy. We need that here."

"You do have to admit that any kids able to get past our security the way they did might just come up with a few clever ideas, at that," added another of the scientists.

"I've already acknowledged that these kids are very impressive," said Dr. Harris. He paused for several long seconds in thought, but finally a frown crept over his face and he shook his head. "But the answer is still no. I believe that—"

"Mom!" shouted Ryan in horror. "Look out!"

A bolt holding a heavy portable generator to the pole above Mrs. Resnick had worked its way lose. Ryan had caught it out of the corner of his eye as it popped free and the generator began its fall—straight down toward his mother's head.

Ryan watched the generator fall in horror, knowing that his warning had been too late to save his mom.

CHAPTER 13

Bug Attack!

Just as Mrs. Resnick was beginning to react to her son's warning the generator completed its fall, smashing into the top of her head with a sickening thud.

"No!" screamed Ryan frantically.

His mom sprawled to the floor, unconscious. Blood was pouring from her head.

The scientists reacted immediately, surrounding her. Tears came to Mr. Resnick's eyes at the sight of his badly injured wife. He tore his shirt from his body and wrapped it around her head like a turban to help staunch the flow of blood, and then gently cradled her head in his arms. Ryan knelt beside him, horrified, while Regan looked on in total shock.

Dr. Harris gave her a quick examination. He didn't even need to say anything; the look on his face was enough. She was in trouble.

"Is she going to make it?" whispered Ben Resnick.

"It doesn't look good," said Dr. Harris grimly. "But if we can get her to a hospital in time she has a small chance."

"Let's move then," said their father, fighting to hold himself together. "Kids, I need you to run as fast as you can back to the elevator. Take it to the top and then send it back down so it'll be waiting for us. Call 9-1-1 and have an ambulance meet us at the main building." He didn't wait for a response. "Go!" he commanded.

The Resnick siblings dashed off, leaving the group by the stairs. But just as they passed into the next room on the way to the outside they were stopped in their tracks by a blood-curdling scream.

They turned back toward the room and were greeted by a sight straight out of a horror movie. An infestation of insects was pouring out of the floor, completely surrounding the group of scientists and their mom. They were pitch black and were the size of very large ants. They had six perfectly identical body segments, and each segment had a pair of both legs and pincers that seemed to be in constant motion. There must have been millions of them; a living sea of relentless alien insects so dense that they were stacked on top of each other, several inches deep. Large chunks of rock had appeared as well, maybe from under the floor, and as the insects swarmed over them on their way to the group of scientists the rocks completely dissolved, like ice-cubes in a pot of boiling water.

The scientists were frantically searching for a way around the swarm, but there wasn't one. They were completely encircled and were even cut off from the staircase.

Both kids froze in horror as they watched. Their father spotted them out of the corner of his eye. "Go!" he shouted from the middle of the sea of hungry insects. "Get out of here!"

"We won't just leave you!" cried Regan.

"This is not a discussion!" he shouted. "You can't help us. You have to save yourselves. Go!"

Both kids still hesitated.

"Go!" screamed their father, louder than he had ever screamed before, and with unmistakable panic in his voice. Ryan saw the pleading look in his eye and realized he was far more afraid for *them* than he was for himself— afraid they wouldn't run to safety as he was desperate to have them do. This alone sparked Ryan into action.

"We'll bring help," he shouted as he sprinted from the room, yanking on his sister's shirt so she would follow. He knew the odds were one in a million that they could bring help back in time, but they had to *try*.

They were halfway to the building's exit when, in his haste, Ryan smashed into a strange, shimmering podium that promptly retracted into the ground and disappeared. Wincing in pain, he put on a burst of speed and caught up with his sister who was now running toward three oval exits. He could have sworn there had only been a single doorway when they had entered. He followed his sister through the center doorway and was relieved to find that they had chosen correctly and it led to the outside.

Ryan looked for the walkway that would help speed them back to the cavern, and possible help, hoping it would still accelerate their pace even when they were running. He was about to sprint onto it when Regan grabbed his arm from behind. "Ryan, wait!"

"What?" he said impatiently, unable to believe his sister was trying to slow him down.

"Remember the blowtorches we saw just outside the room Mom and Dad were in?" she said excitedly. "They were *outside* the circle of bugs. So we can get them! We can use them as weapons on the swarm! I don't care how alien they are, those bugs are bound to be afraid of fire. Come on!"

Ryan's eyes widened. "Great idea!" he said.

They raced back into the building with a renewed sense of hope and purpose. Maybe they *could* save their parents.

They each gathered a blowtorch and shot through the entrance to the staircase room, gasping for breath, their eyes darting across the floor, searching for the best place to begin waging war on the eruption of relentless alien attackers. But what they saw was totally unexpected and took their breath away.

The alien creatures were gone! All of them. And everything else in the room was gone as well.

They looked on in horror, knowing they had been too late. The room was completely empty. Completely.

The insects must have devoured everything in their path.

Not a single trace of their parents or any of the other scientists remained.

CHAPTER 14

Vanishing Act

Ryan raced up the wispy stairs in desperation. He returned moments later and shook his head. No one was on the second floor either.

How could this be happening, he thought in despair.

A tear rolled gently down Regan's cheek. "Could they have escaped out another exit?"

Ryan shook his head sadly. "Those insect things picked the room clean," he whispered woodenly. "Look at it. There's no trace that anyone was ever here. No people, no equipment—nothing. The pole that was leaning against the stairs is gone. There's not even any blood stains where Mom was hit."

"But how could they eat through solid steel, Ryan? How?"

"I don't know," said her brother sullenly. "But you

saw how quickly they devoured solid rock. I guess steel and . . ." he was about to say bone but thought better of it. "I guess steel is no different."

"But we were only gone about two minutes," persisted Regan. "They couldn't be *that* fast. Are you saying they devoured the equipment and all those people and disappeared again in less than two minutes? I don't believe it. Mom and Dad are still alive," she insisted. "I *know* they are. They have to be." And with that she broke into tears.

Ryan wiped away several large tears that had escaped from the corners of his own eyes and put an arm around his sister. He tried to find words to comfort her, but there were none to find.

After a few minutes Regan managed to get her emotions back under control. Her parents *were* alive, she told herself, and she was going to figure out where they were.

She forced herself to concentrate on the room once more. It was uncanny how quiet it now was and even more uncanny how selective the swarm had been. None of the many alien objects in the room had been touched, nor had the stairs, the floor, or the doorways. Nothing. The insects had devoured every last microscopic shred of everything from Earth, people or otherwise, and hadn't touched a single atom of anything that was already here. She pointed this observation out to Ryan. "How did they know?" she asked him. "Why would they prefer Earth stuff?"

"I don't know," he said. "Probably because the alien building material is too tough for them. You saw how tough just those thin strands are."

"But they were able to eat through the floor," Regan pointed out. "Yet there's no trace of any damage to it. Where did they come from? Where did those rock chunks come from? What kind of . . . creatures . . . like to eat metal, plastic, *and* people? And how did they know that Earth stuff wasn't poisonous?"

"You're right. It doesn't make sense."

"Do you think the swarm will return?"

Ryan shuddered. "Let's not wait around to find out."

They retraced their path back to where they had first entered the perilous city in numbed silence. This time, instead of marveling at the fantastic architecture around them they kept their eyes on the ground, searching for the return of the piranha-like insects and trying not to think about the fate of their parents.

Finally, after a period of time that seemed far longer than it really was, they arrived at the edge of the city, to the place at which they had entered. The opaque wall of energy ran in a smooth curve in front of them, distorting their vision. They looked for the swirling colors that would mark the hole in the energy shield that their father had torn open.

It wasn't there! The entrance was gone!

How could that be?

They were trapped!

Trapped in a city that had already shown how deadly it could be.

And who knew how long it would be before the swarm of alien insects became hungry again.

CHAPTER 15

Trapped!

They looked around frantically. There must be some mistake.

"Are we sure this is the right place?" said Regan.

"Positive." Yet where was the opening?

"We're never going to leave here, are we?" whispered Regan.

"Don't be silly. Of course we will," said Ryan, trying hard for his sister's sake to sound far more confident than he felt.

"Maybe the entrance moved," offered Regan. "Carl said the city seemed like a living thing sometimes. We didn't find out what he meant. Maybe parts of the city can move around on their own."

Ryan shook his head. "We've stayed on the walkway all the way back so we know we didn't get lost. This is where we entered. The cavern is a few inches from us and we know it didn't move. If the original entrance moved somehow, the lasers and other machinery in the cavern would have torn another hole here."

They stood in silence for several minutes straining to see an opening in the force-field wall that wasn't there. Ryan felt totally helpless and he had no idea what to do. If only his parents were there. They always knew what to do.

So what *would* they do in this situation?

The answer came to him almost at once. If they were confronted by this puzzle they would try to solve it using a process called the scientific method. His dad had gone over the scientific method with him in great detail just a few months before. First, you observed things. They had done that. They had observed a swarm of deadly insects devour everything human and nothing alien. They had observed that the entrance to the city was gone. Then you formed a hypothesis—some kind of idea that could explain everything you had observed. An idea that would allow you to make predictions, and to design experiments to test these predictions. If the results of your experiments failed to support your predictions, you would have to modify your hypothesis or even throw it away completely. Your goal would be to find a hypothesis that *would* account for all of your observations and allow you to successfully predict the outcome of additional experiments.

To make sure Ryan understood his explanation, his

father had borrowed a feather from an old pillow and marched him into the backyard. Mr. Resnick was soon holding his arms out in front of him over the lawn, at exactly the same height, with the feather in one hand and a large rock in the other. Then he let go of both at the same time. The rock quickly slammed into the grass with a thud while the feather lazily made its way down to earth.

"What did you observe?" asked Mr. Resnick.

"The rock fell faster," said Ryan immediately.

"Do you have a hypothesis that could explain this?"

Ryan rolled his eyes. His dad could have chosen a more difficult example than this. "Heavy objects fall faster than light objects."

"How could you test this hypothesis?"

"There's no need to test it," said Ryan. "In this case it isn't a hypothesis, it's an absolute fact."

"Are you sure about that?" asked Mr. Resnick, his eyes twinkling.

Ryan nodded. "Positive."

His dad grinned broadly. "Let's try it anyway. Show me a way to test the hypothesis."

Ryan found a small pebble and retrieved the same large, heavy rock his dad had dropped. He held them out in front of him, one in each hand, and dropped them with a bored look.

They landed at the exact same time!

Impossible! Ryan couldn't believe his eyes.

Shaking his head in disbelief, Ryan picked up the pebble and rock and tried once again, this time making absolutely certain he released them at the same time, from the exact same height. Sure enough, he had not imagined it—they both hit the ground at the exact same instant.

Ryan still refused to believe it. His father watched, amused, as he tested rubber bands and pebbles and paperclips against basketballs and rocks and phone books. In each case, both of the test objects landed at exactly the same time. *He had been so sure.* All his instincts told him the heavy objects would fall faster. But they didn't.

Ryan winced, feeling a little foolish. "Okay, maybe I'm not as positive as I thought."

His dad smiled. "Okay, so your original hypothesis is wrong, after all. Good thing we did the experiments. Can you think of a hypothesis that *does* account for all of the results?"

Ryan thought about it. The only object he had tried that didn't fit the pattern was the feather. It was the oddball. He dropped the feather by itself a few times and watched it carefully. It didn't take long for him to realize that it was the *air* that was slowing it down. Finally, he had his new hypothesis. "All objects fall at exactly the same speed," he said, "*unless* one of the objects is light enough to float in the air."

His dad encouraged him to come up with an experiment to test this new hypothesis, and Ryan rose to the challenge. He taped several pieces of facial tissue together until they weighed exactly the same as a paperclip and dropped them both. Sure enough, the paperclip cut through the air and landed quickly while the tissues floated slowly to the ground.

His dad had suggested another test would be to drop a feather and a bowling ball on the moon, which had no air. If this hypothesis was correct, on the moon the feather and the bowling ball, against all human expectations, should both land at the exact same time.

Ryan remembered vividly how his father had congratulated him and confirmed that his new hypothesis was, indeed, correct and that sure enough, all objects on a given planet *did* fall at exactly the same speed *as long as there wasn't any air to slow the objects down.*

The scientific method was simple but it had been responsible for huge advances in scientific knowledge. Could Ryan apply it here? Maybe. An idea began to form in his head.

"Wait a second," he said finally, breaking the long silence. "Let's imagine the city *is* alive, like an enormous animal." He had been about to say, 'let's *hypothesize* the city is alive' but didn't want to risk confusing his sister. "If we were inside a city-sized animal, what would that make us?"

"Lunch?" guessed Regan.

Ryan shook his head. "No, we'd be far smaller than a crumb. Think much, much smaller."

It took Regan only seconds to see the answer. "A disease," she said confidently. Their mom was a biologist and had taught them well.

"Right. So imagine the force-field surrounding the city is like our skin—our first line of defense against invaders. The best way to avoid an infection is to not let it enter the body in the first place. Our skin helps prevent an invasion by bacteria, maybe the force-field is there to prevent invasion by . . . well, maybe invasion by . . . us."

Regan frowned. "Maybe. But if that's true, it failed. We did get in. We cut the city's shield."

"Right," said Ryan. "But what happens when *we* get a cut?"

"Lots of things," said Regan, not sure what he was getting at.

"Our skin eventually heals. It grows back and *fills in the gap*."

Now she saw where he was going with this. This could explain why the entrance was gone—the barrier managed to heal itself.

"And what happens *after* bacteria enter the body?" continued Ryan excitedly.

Their mother had explained this many times. "The body's defense force comes into action," replied Regan. "The body's immune system—antibodies and other cells. They kill the bacteria."

"Right. And the antibodies can tell which cells are

part of your body and which cells are foreign. Anything the immune system doesn't identify as part of your body is targeted for elimination." He paused. "Sound familiar?"

It did! This theory would also explain why human stuff was devoured and alien stuff was left alone. If the bugs' job was to protect the city from invaders, they would only attack the invaders.

"But why now?" said Regan. "Humans have been in the city now for more than a day."

"It can take a while for the immune army to build, especially when facing something totally new," said her brother. "Sometimes the immune system isn't fast enough and the bacteria multiply so much that they win the battle for a while and you get sick."

"It is a great theory, Ryan. It does explain a lot. But then why haven't they attacked *us* yet?"

Good question. Ryan was about to say, *I wish I knew,* when the answer hit him. Of course! "Because the scientists damaged the inside of the city," he said. "They cut a piece of the webbing from that staircase. They actively attacked it. If something does that to our body the damaged part sends out all kinds of chemical signals that can activate the immune system." He paused. "Even though people are foreign to the city, we must seem pretty harmless, so it isn't too worried about us. But as soon as the scientists cut that piece of material out the city saw us as a danger and sent out the army."

This had to be right, thought Regan. How else to

explain the insect attack only minutes after the webbing was cut. "So if we concentrate on being totally harmless . . ." she began.

"Then we won't attract them," finished Ryan. "Exactly. We just have to be sure to be very gentle. Don't even disturb a single flower," he cautioned.

Damaging the city on purpose would be a great way to test his hypothesis, but then again, if he *was* right, it would also be a great way to get himself devoured by the city's 'antibodies'. This was one hypothesis he wasn't so eager to test at the moment.

A tear rolled gently down Regan's face as she thought once again of her parents. If only their mom could be with them to see how well they had paid attention to her lessens in biology.

Ryan knew he couldn't afford to consider his parents' fate right now. He was determined to get his sister to safety and they were still trapped in a very dangerous alien city. His parents wouldn't want him to just give up. They would want him to do whatever it took to save himself and his sister.

"We need to explore the city," said Ryan in determination. "We have to find a way out, or maybe some alien equipment we can use to open another hole in the shield. And we need to find food and water, too. We may be here a long time."

Not finding food and drink was Ryan's biggest fear. They would have to keep exploring individual buildings until they did. People could last a long time without food if they had to, but the human body couldn't get by without water for very long at all.

"Let's go," said Ryan, pretending to be confident. He was determined to find a way out of here somehow.

But he didn't have the faintest idea how he could accomplish this impossible task.

CHAPTER 16

Technology and Magic

Ryan and Regan explored for hour after hour as their hunger and thirst mounted—and their desperation.

They went into several structures and discovered artifacts of every size, shape and kind. They inspected several very cautiously but couldn't figure out how to operate any of them—or even if they *could* be operated. It was maddening. For all they knew they had held the key to leaving the city in their hands and hadn't recognized it.

Dr. Harris had said current human technology would seem like magic to earlier ages. So what would a prehistoric man make of the inside of their house? Would he think a telephone hanging on a wall was art? That a computer was something used for hunting—to throw at animals? What would he make of a microwave oven? He could be in total darkness, searching frantically for some flint to hit together to make a fire, not knowing that all he had to do was push the small white switches sticking out from the walls and he could have all the light he needed. What if he was hungry? He could find a can of soup and never know there was food inside. Even if he did, he wouldn't know what a can-opener was or how to use it. A feast could be waiting inside the refrigerator but he wouldn't guess it, and he wouldn't even know for sure that a refrigerator could even be *opened*.

Ryan and Regan knew that in this case, *they* were the ignorant primitives stumbling around in the dark, not advanced enough to have any idea of what they were seeing within the astonishing alien buildings.

Ryan continued to try to put on a brave face for his sister but he was getting more worried by the hour. "If we ever get out of here," he said and then quickly amended, "I mean—*when* we get out of here, I promise to never complain about being bored again."

Regan smiled weakly as they exited another building after yet another fruitless search. "Yeah. I'd give anything to be bored right now. This could have been the greatest day of our lives. Getting to see this amazing city. Learning about the most important discovery of all time. But instead, it's turned into a nightmare. How could things—"

"Down!" screamed Ryan.

Before Regan could react he dove on her and threw her forcefully to the soft ground, covering her with his body.

Regan looked up in terror to find the reason for her brother's action.

An immense alien bird of prey was flying directly toward them! It had the sleek, dangerous lines of an eagle, but it was the size of a *minivan*.

The swooping predator extended its razor sharp talons as it prepared to complete its attack.

CHAPTER 17

The Unearthly Zoo

Regan closed her eyes tightly.
A few seconds went by.

Then a few more. Confused but relieved, Regan opened her eyes.

The bird was gone! In its place was a small, cuddly-looking alien creature with big blue eyes. "What in the world . . ." she began.

As she watched, wide-eyed, the creature vanished, only to be replaced by an animal that looked something like a kangaroo with the face of a lion.

"Holograms," whispered Ryan. Although the animals looked every bit as real as his sister did, they weren't. None of them. They were just three-dimensional movies.

He quickly got to his feet and helped Regan up off the ground. "Are you okay?" he asked.

She ignored his question. "You saved my life," she whispered, her eyes wide. "And you risked your own life to do it. I really owe you one."

"Nah," said Ryan, feeling awkward at his sister's heartfelt appreciation. "I just haven't tackled you in a while and thought this would be a good excuse. I only saved you from a hologram," he finished modestly.

"You didn't know that at the time, so I'm afraid you're stuck being a hero," she insisting in a tone that made it clear that this was the final word on the subject.

As they talked, perfect three-dimensional holograms of different animals continued to appear before them. The images changed every few seconds and they had yet to start repeating. The animals appeared directly in front of a large, arch-shaped building.

"A zoo?" guessed Regan after watching several more animal holograms appear.

"That would make sense," said Ryan. "But inside this single building? The cages would have to be awfully small."

"Even if it is—or was—a zoo," said Regan, "it's not as though any animals are still going to be alive in there. This city has been abandoned for a long, long time."

They had been in the city all day and had yet to find the slightest hint that the city had *ever* been inhabited.

"Let's check it out anyway," suggested Ryan.

They entered to find that the building contained absolutely nothing but dozens of oval doorways, spaced evenly around the walls. Above each doorway a different animal hologram appeared every few seconds, just as they had outside. This time the holograms above each doorway seemed to have a theme; winter animals, or desert animals, and each of the groupings had subtle similarities that made the kids think they came from the same planet.

Regan gestured to one of the doorways. It was clear they could pass through the opening but they couldn't see what was on the other side. "Should we go through one of them?"

Ryan considered. "Okay, but I'll go first," he said protectively. He walked through a doorway with his sister close behind.

They had expected to see cages. What they saw was a vast forest of trees with greenish bark and round, orange leaves. A forest that was far, far larger than the entire building they were in! Maybe even larger than the entire *city*.

"These nutty aliens," quipped Regan. "They really do *wonderful* things with living space. I'd love to have them design a closet for me—with a thousand times more room inside than the house it's in."

"Ah, I think they could even do better than that," whispered Ryan in a trance. He pointed upward.

Upward to the sky and the clouds. They were outside!

Incredible! And even more incredible was the fact

that they could see two huge orbs hanging in the sky, visible even during the day.

Moons! And there were two of them!

They looked once again at the bizarre orange trees and gulped. They were definitely outside all right.

And they were just as definitely no longer on Earth.

CHAPTER 18

Predator

A terrifying thought occurred to them both at the same time—was the doorway still there? They turned slowly, fearfully, to look behind them. It was! What a relief.

Just to be sure they weren't stranded they stepped through it once more. Sure enough, they were back in the zoo.

They stepped through to the forest again and considered the vast landscape carefully. "I have to admit, the cages are slightly bigger than I thought they would be," said Ryan impishly.

Regan laughed.

"This could be the break we've been looking for," said Ryan. "There must be some sort of food and water here. I think we should stay fairly close to this entrance and explore. Each doorway in the zoo must go to a different world, so if we can't find water right away we can try one of the other worlds."

They decided to climb a nearby tree to scout the area, but after walking only thirty yards a wall of force, just like the one around the city, appeared magically in front of them, completely blocking out the woods. They jumped back, startled.

And the wall disappeared again.

After just a little experimentation it became clear that an invisible dome completely encircled them, with the door back to the city at its center. Whenever they got to within five feet of the barrier it instantly became visible, probably so no one would slam into it without realizing it.

"I suppose this is here so the zoo animals won't eat the zoo visitors," said Ryan.

Regan nodded. "Yeah—probably. Zookeepers must hate it when the animals spoil their appetite that way."

"Well, I guess this is a great setup if you want to safely watch the local animals, but if you want to find food and water—it's not so great."

"I'm not so sure it's so great for watching animals," said Regan. "Do you see any? They could be anywhere on this planet." She shook her head. "What they need is a car or tram of some sort to carry visitors around, like they had in the first *Jurassic Park* movie." She paused. "In fact, I'll bet you they *do* have one somewhere. They would almost *have* to."

Ryan shook his head. "Just because they had a tram in a science fiction movie doesn't mean they'll have one in an alien zoo on an alien planet," he said skeptically. He thought the chances of them finding a tram simply because his sister thought there *should* be one were less than zero. But after looking at his sister's eager face he added, "I guess there isn't harm in looking."

Less than two minutes later they found a tram, right where Regan had guessed it would be. Ryan stared at it in disbelief and whispered, "You were right. Nice going. Let's just hope we don't find the *dinosaurs* from that movie here also," he joked.

They entered the small tram carefully. Inside several small holograms showed the tram performing different maneuvers. Ryan reached forward and touched one that showed the tram going forward. As he had hoped, it served as a control, and the actual tram began to glide slowly forward into the unknown woods. It passed beyond the location of the force-field without activating it.

Minutes later they exited the tram and climbed one of the orange trees. They were in luck! A stream was only a few hundred yards away, winding its way through the woods.

Using the holographic controls they drove toward the stream. The tram slid forward as though on a sheet of ice, even over rough and uneven terrain. They passed several small alien animals but nothing that looked threatening.

They parked the tram and walked eagerly to the stream. Ryan bent over and put a hand in. The water was cool and nothing had ever looked more refreshing. He smelled it carefully. It had no odor of any kind. This was a good sign. Ryan cupped his hands and prepared to take a sip.

"Shouldn't we test it first?" said Regan. "To be sure it really *is* water. We're not on Earth, after all."

"I already tested it the only way I know how. It feels and smells exactly like water," said Ryan.

"And it probably is. But what if it turns out to be some strange liquid that doesn't exist on Earth? For all we know, a single drop might kill us."

Ryan looked at his hands nervously and then quickly wiped them dry on his pants. "Okay. That's a good point," he acknowledged. His forehead creased in thought. "So how else do you test for water?"

"I have no idea?"

"But you were the one who just said we should test it."

"I know," she said. "Since I came up with the idea, I thought you could come up with the test," she added, smiling.

Ryan laughed. "Okay," he said. "I accept the challenge." He thought for a moment. "I guess the key is to think of properties of water that are unique."

"Are there any?"

"Yeah. I know I learned that water is pretty remarkable, either from Mom or at school. Give me a minute to remember." He strained as hard as he could until some of the information finally began to come back to him. "Okay," he began. "Here's a unique property. Things expand when they get warmer and contract when they get colder. Like the liquid in a thermometer. So if you freeze a liquid solid, it contracts: it takes up less space. But water does the *opposite*," he added triumphantly. "Water actually *expands* when it's frozen."

Very interesting, thought Regan. She remembered leaving a bottle of water in the freezer a few months earlier. Sure enough, when it had turned to ice it had expanded and broken the bottle. She hadn't really thought about it before, but he was right.

"And because water expands when it freezes," continued her brother, "ice is less dense than water, so it's able to *float* on water. This floating thing is very unique to water also."

"So what are you saying, that if you made ice-cubes out of gasoline and put them in a *glass* of gasoline, the cubes would sink to the bottom?"

"Exactly," he said. He smiled as an image popped into his head of a woman in a fancy dress, sipping a glass of cold gasoline like it was lemonade. "I remember Mom telling me that this was a very important property of water. Because ice floats, in the winter a lake or river becomes frozen on top, protecting the water beneath from freezing also. If ice didn't float, the surface would keep freezing and sinking to the bottom until the entire lake or river ended up as a gigantic cube of ice, killing all the fish."

Regan listened in fascination. There had to be a way to use this information. And then it hit her! *Of course.* "You did it Ryan. We have our test. All we have to do is turn some of this stream 'water' into ice and see if it floats in the stream."

"Good plan, Regan, but unless you happen to have a freezer with you it doesn't help us."

Regan grinned broadly. "You've been in California too long, Ryan," she teased. "It's true that in San Diego the only way to freeze water is with a freezer. But in other parts of the country there is another way—*leave it outside during the winter.*"

Ryan laughed. Maybe he *had* lived in California too long. He still couldn't see how this helped them. The answer suddenly dawned on him as it had on his sister and his mouth dropped open. He hadn't adjusted his thinking to the possibilities of the alien city. In the zoo they had instant access to dozens of worlds, several of which would be cold enough to freeze water. Using an entire world as a freezer seemed a bit excessive, but a good scientist had to be able to use whatever tools were available.

Regan could see that he had caught on. "We'll need to go back to the city and find a small container that will hold liquid. Then we can drop it off on an ice-planet and come back after it's frozen."

Ryan nodded. "If it floats in the stream, we'll drink some. It still might not be pure water, but it's the best we can do."

"I agree," said Regan. "What about possible diseases?"

"We'll just have to be careful," her brother replied. "Provided the ice floats, we can drink a very small amount. If that doesn't kill us by tomorrow then we'll know it's okay."

"And if it *does* kill us by tomorrow?" said Regan.

"Then we won't be *thirsty,* will we," responded Ryan with a straight face.

"Very comforting," said Regan.

They turned away from the stream and headed back for the tram. They were halfway there when they spotted their first large animal.

And it spotted them.

It was about five feet tall and probably weighed nine-hundred pounds—with most of this weight in the form of dense, rippling muscle. Its mouth was packed with dagger-like teeth. It was orange and black and looked somewhat reptilian. It had eight powerful legs, four on each side, and each foot ended in a claw that a raptor would envy. It was a vicious predator; an unstoppable killing machine.

And it was between them and the tram.

They froze in place, their breath stuck in their throats. If this beast attacked, it would cut them both to ribbons before they could even blink.

Regan's mind worked furiously. Was there any way out of this? They couldn't possibly outrun it. Besides, running was a very bad idea. Kids who hiked in California were taught that if they encountered a cougar, also known as a mountain lion, the last thing they should do is run, because running only made them look like prey.

What else could they do? They were no match for this alien monster physically. But then, humans had *never* been a match, physically, for any of the predators they had conquered. Only their superior brainpower had allowed them to become the top predator on Earth.

The creature stared at them for several long seconds, trying to figure out what to make of them. Finally, satisfied that they would make easy prey, it snarled fiercely and started toward them with a killer's gleam in its eye, preparing to attack.

And with the immense strength and physical weapons available to the creature one thing was certain; at this moment, all the human brainpower in the universe wasn't going to stop it for even a second.

CHAPTER 19

The Swarm

Suddenly, Regan had an inspiration.

She picked up a large rock by her feet. "Brace yourself, Ryan!" she yelled. And then she did something her brother would never have expected in a million years. She jumped on his back.

Despite her warning he barely managed not to fall over as she climbed up his back and sat on his shoulders. What was she doing?

"Now growl and scream at it!" said Regan, who immediately took her own advice. While they were screaming she threw the rock as hard as she could at the snarling monster, hitting it in the center of its body.

They continued growling and yelling as loudly and fiercely as they could, feeling ridiculous trying to scare this formidable beast with their yells and puny human teeth.

The creature stopped seven feet from them and considered. It studied them carefully for about fifteen seconds while they continued to shout insults at it and then, thinking better of it, hastily retreated back into the woods.

Ryan couldn't believe it! But he wasn't about to wait around to see if the creature was really gone for good. He raced for the safety of the tram, not even stopping to remove Regan from his shoulders until they arrived. They entered the vehicle and quickly began driving back the way they had come.

"Regan, that was *brilliant*. I thought we were goners for sure. Then, when you hit it with that rock, I thought we were *double* goners." He shook his head. "And I also thought you'd totally lost your mind. How did you know that would work?"

"I didn't," she responded simply. "But I know it works with coyotes and cougars and I thought it might work with this thing."

Coyotes and cougars. Ryan had forgotten about that. When you saw one of these animals you were supposed to look as large and threatening as possible so they wouldn't think you were an easy meal. "Okay, but a coyote or a cougar is like a *bunny rabbit* compared to that thing. What made you think it would work on *that* monster?"

"I guessed it had never seen a human before. That

thing has to be used to animals running away from it. So when we changed from two small, unknown animals, into a bigger, two-headed animal, and instead of running actually had the nerve to yell at it, it became confused. Just as I hoped, it wasn't very smart and decided not to take the risk that we were tougher than we looked."

Ryan laughed. "Just about anything would be tougher than we *looked*. My guess is that a pair of bunny rabbit *slippers* are tougher than we *looked*." He paused. "But you can't argue with success. You were absolutely right. Nice going!"

Regan beamed. "Thanks. Who'd have ever thought that Pennsylvania could be this exciting."

"Or this far away from Earth, for that matter," joked Ryan.

They traveled back to the door leading to the alien city in reasonably good spirits. Outsmarting a carnivorous alien creature instead of becoming its meal could cheer anyone up. After searching through several buildings they found a few things that could serve as containers and carried out their experiment, staying closer to the tram this time and keeping more alert for dangerous animals. It worked. The ice floated in the stream. They congratulated each other, took a few sips of water and then returned to the city.

They wandered through the city for several more

hours and were surprised to find that the lighting dimmed gradually. The city must have been set to the same cycle of light and dark as the Earth. Finally it was dark and they realized they were exhausted. They found a stretch of soft ground and slept soundly through the night.

When they awoke the next morning, both hunger and thirst gnawed at them painfully. But so far the water hadn't had any ill effects. They would wait a little longer and return to the wooded planet for more.

They traveled for about an hour when they ran across another building with a holographic display at its front. The building was shaped like a perfectly cut diamond and it sparkled just as brilliantly. The hologram showed a large triangle facing a semicircle of tiny triangles. Behind the large triangle was a separate holographic image of a solar system in space.

Ryan guessed the holograms in front of buildings must serve the same purpose as signs in front of public buildings on Earth. The display in front of the zoo building had identified it quite nicely. "What do you think this building is?" he asked Regan.

Regan studied the hologram. "I'll bet it's a school," she said finally. "The big triangle represents the teacher and the little ones the students."

Ryan nodded. "It could be." Why not? After finding the tram he was beginning to respect his sister's instincts. He gestured toward the entrance. "Let's find out."

They entered a room that contained several ordered rows of solid, tan-colored cubes, about three feet high. On a raised platform next to each cube sat a glass sphere about the size of a softball. They picked one up and examined it, but as usual couldn't figure out its function or purpose.

Regan put her hand on the side of one of the large cubes. It was smooth and very hard. She decided to sit on it and rest her feet.

She gasped as the hard surface completely gave way under her weight and engulfed her. It was as if the material had turned to liquid for just an instant, had surrounded her, and then had hardened again.

"Are you okay?" asked Ryan in alarm.

"I . . . I guess I'm fine," she said in surprise. A smile slowly formed on her face. "You *gotta* try this. This is the most comfortable chair I've ever been in. Like floating in water—or maybe Jello—only better."

"But how will you get out of it?" asked Ryan.

She frowned. "I don't know." She tried to change position—and the chair *let* her. As soon as she moved it reliquefied—not hindering her movement at all—and then solidified again when she stopped moving for a few seconds. As they had come to expect of things associated with the city, it was quite remarkable.

Ryan sat on the cube next to her and it gently engulfed him as it had his sister. Regan was right. The chair was impossibly comfortable. He wondered if there was a way for it to massage his back while he sat. Probably.

He looked to the front of the room and was surprised to see the same holographic image they had seen outside; a large triangle surrounded by smaller ones. He decided to inspect it more closely.

As he got up he stumbled over his own feet. Instinctively he grabbed for the raised platform beside him as he fell and was able to right himself. That was a relief.

"Are you okay?" asked Regan.

"Fine," he replied. As he answered he noticed that the glass globe that had been sitting on the platform he had just grabbed had slowly rolled to the edge and was teetering there. He lunged for it. Too late. The globe fell to the floor and smashed into dozens of pieces.

Regan winced but then shrugged her shoulders. "Look on the bright side. At least no one is here to miss it, whatever it was. I wouldn't worry about—"

She stopped in mid-sentence, horrified. They had forgotten about the city's immune system. Would the destruction of the globe somehow alert the city's defense force again? From the look on Ryan's face it was clear he had also realized the danger they were in. "Let's get out of here!" he urged.

Regan screamed.

It was too late. Their worst fears had been realized.

A swarm of the black, piranha-like insects erupted through the floor with astonishing speed, totally surrounding them in seconds. Millions of pairs of tiny insect legs clicked furiously on the ground and millions of pairs of mandibles gnashed together horribly.

The siblings watched in terror and revulsion as the unstoppable wave of death advanced steadily toward them.

CHAPTER 20

Repairs

The insects fell upon a few of the broken pieces of the globe, which immediately melted away under their ever-moving jaws.

Ryan and Regan held on to each other, helpless, and braced for the end.

The insects cut a careful path around them to get to the other pieces of the globe.

Around them?

Ryan saw an opening! In their present formation he might just be able to jump beyond the swarm. He launched himself forward with all of his might.

He realized with a sickening feeling that he wasn't going to make it.

But just as he was about to land on thousands of the insects at the edge of the swarm they scattered, leaving him an open space.

Could it be! He took a step toward the center of the swarm.

And they scattered once again. Again, his foot landed on empty floor.

"Look," he yelled excitedly to Regan. "They're not trying to eat us. They're *avoiding* us."

In seconds Regan had verified what her brother had said. In fact, it was *impossible* to touch one of the scurrying insects. They managed to completely avoid the two kids while going about their business of devouring every piece of the strange broken globe. And then, while Ryan and Regan looked on in astonishment, thousands of the bugs packed themselves into a tight ball. They stayed in this position for only a few seconds and then fell away again to reveal a perfect, intact, glass globe.

Ryan's hypothesis had been tested, after all, *and it was wrong*. The insects weren't the *defense* crew. They were the *repair* crew.

Ryan could tell from the look on his sister's face that she had reached the same conclusion he had. Although he still hadn't entirely lost his fear of the ferocious looking creatures, he decided to bend down to get a closer look at them. But as he began to do so the bugs chewed several holes in the floor and scurried into them, almost faster than his eyes could follow. The holes instantly filled up again to match the rest of the floor, and other than the repaired globe, no sign remained that the insects were ever there.

Unbelievable.

"You know what this means," said Regan in elation. "It means that Mom and Dad and the other scientists are alive! Those things *couldn't* have eaten them."

Ryan's eyes widened. Regan was absolutely right! He allowed himself a glimmer of hope for the first time since the group of Prometheus scientists had disappeared.

But Regan's spirits sank once again as she remembered her mom's desperate condition. "They must have found out the bugs wouldn't hurt them and ran to take Mom to the hospital. By the time we got back, they and the bugs were gone."

"We never even looked to see if they'd repaired the staircase," said Ryan. Knowing that the bugs were the repair crew and not the defense crew cleared up several mysteries, but many others remained. "But this still doesn't explain what happened to all the *equipment* in the room," he pointed out. "Or how so many people could have left a room so quickly while carrying Mom," he added. "And we still don't know where they are and why the entrance to the city is gone."

"Maybe not," said Regan, "but things are certainly looking up. It would be a lot harder for us to solve these mysteries if we were bug food right now."

Ryan smiled. "You've definitely got a point there," he admitted.

"Let's get out of here," she suggested.

Ryan eyed the hologram floating in space, now only

a few feet in front of him. This had been his goal when he had left the chair in the first place. "Okay," he said. "But I want to try something first. Holograms were used as controls for that tram we were in. Maybe these are controls too." He walked over to the hologram and touched the image of the large triangle suspended in air.

They gasped in alarm as the hologram disappeared and they were suddenly floating in deep space, surrounded by nothing but endless blackness and billions of stars.

Where were they!

They couldn't survive in deep space!

It gradually dawned on them that they hadn't *gone* anywhere. Their surroundings were just a perfect illusion. The small hologram with the triangles had just been replaced by a far larger one of deep space, extending as far as they could see in every direction. It totally surrounded them and was breathtakingly realistic.

Suddenly the holographic galaxy raced past them, although it seemed to them that *they* were the ones moving—hurtling toward a tiny grouping of stars at unimaginable speed. After only a few seconds the hologram came to an abrupt halt. In front of them, far off in the starry distance, two glowing, semi-molten planets of different sizes were hurtling toward each other. They collided an instant later, unleashing more energy in few terrible seconds than a billion nuclear bombs. A massive spray of matter exploded thousands of miles into space as the planets liquefied further and became a single, sun-like body.

Their perspective shifted again. This time a large planetary body floated in front of them encircled by spectacular rings. It could well have been Saturn.

"Hello, children," a disembodied voice said gently in perfect English. *"Do you like the view?"*

For some reason, the voice didn't startle either of them. And it should have. But there was something else that was strange about the voice, thought Ryan. What was it?

A chill went up his spine as he realized the truth. The words had not been spoken aloud. They had been spoken directly into his mind! In fact, he could feel an unmistakably foreign presence and a strange tingle in his brain. Whatever had spoken to them had used telepathy.

"Who are you?" stammered Ryan nervously.

"Why . . . I'm the Teacher, of course," answered the voice. There was a pause. *"What would you like to learn today?"*

CHAPTER 21

The Universe-Wide-Web

Ryan's jaw dropped open. His sister had been right again! This *was* a schoolhouse.

"Regan," he said, "are you ah ... *hearing* this also?"

Regan nodded.

"I use mental telepathy, but you both 'hear' the same thing," explained the Teacher.

"Where are you?" asked Ryan.

"I'm interwoven into the fabric of this city. You might think of me as a computer, although one far more advanced and evolved than the simple computers that humans have so far developed. You can ask me anything you like and I will try and answer if I can."

"How do you know English?" asked Regan.

"I know it because you know it."

Ryan digested this answer for a moment and then asked, "Why are we surrounded by a hologram of space?"

"I thought you might appreciate the beauty and majesty of your galaxy. And I wanted to give you the chance to see what many of your scientists consider the most important event in the history of the formation of your planet and moon." There was a pause. *"Also, floating in space can be quite calming."*

The Teacher was absolutely right about two of its three statements, thought Regan, as their surroundings continued to gently morph from one view of stars, galaxies, and planets to another: each more spectacular than the last. Space was indescribably beautiful, and the illusion of floating in the infinite majesty of the cosmos *was* calming. But she was sure she had misunderstood the Teacher's other statement. "Wait a second," she said. "Are you saying that the collision we just saw was between the Earth and the Moon?"

"No. It was a simulation of the most popular theory among your scientists as to how your moon was formed. It's called the 'Giant Impact Hypothesis'. The idea is that 4.5 billion years ago, a planet the size of Mars smashed into your planet. The debris from the collision eventually gathered into orbit around Earth and later formed your moon."

"That's really what happened?" said Ryan in awe.

"It hasn't been absolutely proven," answered the Teacher. *"But a majority of your scientists certainly believe this is the case."*

To think that a cataclysmic event of this magnitude had really happened, and had been responsible for the creation of the moon, was very, very cool. Ryan wondered why he had never learned this before, and was dying to know more, but decided he needed to ask more pressing questions. "What is this city?" he said. "And can you tell us how it got here?"

"This is an observation post. It was built by a race called the Qwervy. The Qwervy seed these around the galaxy on planets that they think have promising species on them. They visit them occasionally to check on their progress—say once every hundred years. When a species has achieved a certain level of maturity, the Qwervy make themselves known."

"Is humanity mature enough yet?" asked Ryan.

"I'm afraid not. Although you are making much faster progress than the Qwervy ever thought you would. You have tremendous potential as a species. The fact that your species found this outpost and found a way to get inside is remarkable—and quite unexpected."

"Hold on a second," complained Regan. "You're telling us that this gigantic city is an observation post that is only visited every hundred years. Why would they build an entire huge, elaborate city just for that?"

"Why not? It's just as easy for the Qwervy to build a city this size as it is to build a small building."

"What?" said Regan. "How is that possible?" She realized at just that instant that her head was beginning to feel funny, as if her brain was running a marathon and was becoming fatigued, sore, and even overheated. From the slightly pained expression on her brother's face she guessed that he was feeling the same way.

"Oh, they don't build anything themselves," answered the Teacher. *"They use what you would call nano-robots."*

Suddenly they were no longer in space. Instead, they were standing in front of a hologram of a six-foot model of the insects they had encountered twice. Magnified in this way they could now see that their bodies were really made up of tiny gears and motors and their mandibles, antenna, and mouths were all obviously precision tools of unknown types.

"The insects aren't alive," gasped Ryan in amazement. "They're miniature robots."

"Exactly. Nano-robots. 'Nano' essentially means very small. In fact, the Qwervy have invented nano-robots billions of times smaller even than these. Your scientists are attempting to do the same. When the Qwervy visit a planet that has a promising species, they drop one of these off. It builds the city for them."

"Did you say one?" said Regan. "They drop *one* of these off?"

"*That's correct. One. A single nano-robot tunnels deep into the ground. It uses whatever it finds as food—rocks and things—and converts these raw materials into whatever it needs to build an exact copy of itself. It then makes the copy and you get two nano-robots. They both do the same, eat rock and make exact copies of themselves, and then you have four of them.*"

"How can they convert something like rock into everything they need to build tiny, complex robots?" asked Ryan.

"*Why not? Your body does the same thing with the food you eat. Food gives you energy, yes, but it is also the only source of building material for your body. You have to grow from a tiny baby into an adult. Somewhere in the ice-cream, peanut butter, pizza and broccoli that you eat your body finds the raw materials it needs to make muscle cells and heart cells and brain cells. Although I have to admit,*" teased the Teacher, "*I'm detecting far less evidence that either of you use broccoli as a raw material than the other foods I mentioned.*"

Both kids smiled broadly.

"*In any event,*" concluded the Teacher, "*you should be aware that part of your current body used to be mashed potatoes and popcorn.*"

"I guess that's true," said Ryan, absentmindedly rubbing his temples and trying to ignore the increasing discomfort in his brain. "I never really thought about it that way."

"The nano-robots keep eating rock and converting it into more of themselves in this way until there are trillions of them—it doesn't take long."

"Trillions?" said Ryan in disbelief.

"Again I ask you, why not? Your body started from a single cell and you have trillions of cells in you. It's called exponential growth. If you start with a penny and double what you have every day, so you have two cents tomorrow, four cents the next day, eight cents the next, and so on, you would have more than a dollar on the eighth day and more than a million dollars in less than thirty days. Try it on a calculator sometime."

The hologram of the nano-robot disappeared and was replaced by a movie of the nano-robots building the city. *"After a large enough number of them are made, they convert rock and dirt and other materials they find in the ground into what they need to build the city. The entire set of instructions they need are programmed into each one of them."*

The hologram of multiplying nano-robots now surrounded them. The tiny workers ate and multiplied at fantastic speeds. Every so often huge numbers of them would split off from the main swarm and perform a specific job like digging, or construction, or waste removal.

"This is exactly what happens in our bodies, isn't it?" said Ryan excitedly. "Mom explained it to me. Every cell in our body has the programming to make an entire person. A person starts from just one cell and as that one divides and makes more, at some point, following their instructions, the cells start doing different jobs. Some become heart cells, and some become eye cells and so on."

"Exactly. So you see, the Qwervy just have to drop off one nano-robot and leave. The nano-robot does the rest. It doesn't take any extra effort on their part, and they get to stay in a full-blown city when they come to visit. Just as it would take the same effort on your part to grow a single blade of grass or a mighty oak tree—just stick a seed into the ground and walk away. The programming in the seed takes care of the rest."

Both kids listened in fascination to the Teacher. It was able to explain things in a way that made them simple to understand.

"After the nano-robots have finished building the city, a number of them remain to carry out maintenance, cleaning and repairs."

"Boy, I would sure love to have a few thousand of those things to clean my room," said Regan. "Except that they do kind of give me the creeps."

"The Qwervy will be sorry to hear that," thought the Teacher playfully. *"They actually like the little things. You know, they could easily program them to look like tiny, pink teddy-bears if they wanted to."*

Fascinating, thought Ryan. Was there anything the Qwervy *couldn't* do?

"So how can the city be so much bigger inside than it is outside?" asked Regan, turning to another subject. "And we were on an entirely different planet after going through a doorway in the zoo building. How is *that* possible?"

"I'm afraid you wouldn't be able to understand the exact mechanism behind it. The Qwervy can tap into other dimensions and can link one world to another."

The Teacher scanned their minds carefully once again to find a better way to explain how the cities were arranged. *"You are familiar with the Internet, correct?"* Not waiting for an answer the Teacher continued. *"The Internet links computers, and the information inside of them, together in a huge and complex web. Ryan, can you tell me how you navigate on the web?"*

"Sure. It's easy. The information on the web is laid out in web pages. Each one has its own address. And most web pages contain links inside of them to other web pages. By clicking on a link, you immediately travel to the other web page."

"Good. So think of this city as a web page in a massive Internet. Only this one connects planets, not computer information. The doorways you walked through in the zoo were links. Links to other worlds. And each of these worlds are also linked to other worlds. In this way millions of planets are linked together."

"So it's not a World-Wide-Web, it's a Universe-Wide-Web," noted Ryan.

"*Exactly. Instead of surfing web-pages, the Qwervy surf planets.*"

"Incredible," said Ryan.

"Do they ever come here?" asked Regan.

"*I'm afraid not. Only the few Qwervy responsible for checking on Earth's progress. This planet has restricted access. Surfers can only come to planets that don't have intelligent life or are populated by mature species that are active members in the web. Hopefully someday you'll be ready to become part of this galactic community, but you aren't yet.*"

"But how do . . ." began Regan before her question was interrupted by the Teacher.

"*Sorry to interrupt, but I'm afraid we're out of time. Your brain cells are not reacting well to my presence. If I stay in contact with you much longer I will overstimulate your brains and cause permanent damage.*"

Ryan realized that his brain *did* feel as though it were about to explode. The painful side-effects of the mental connection to the Teacher were accelerating rapidly.

"*If you would like me to contact you again, there may be a way, but I will need your permission. I will need to take a perfect and complete copy of your minds. When our connection is broken I can analyze these copies to try to find a precise telepathic frequency that your brains can tolerate. But there is no guarantee I will succeed. The brain of an intelligent being is almost infinitely complex.*"

"It seems worth a try. But why do you need our permission?" asked Regan.

"Because in order to succeed I will need to explore every last thought and memory you have ever had. I will come to understand the true essence of your personalities far better than you can imagine. Some beings feel that this is too great an invasion of their privacy."

Ryan glanced at his sister and raised his eyebrows. "The fact that you could have done this without our permission or knowledge, but didn't, makes me think our privacy will be in good ... ah ... hands," finished Ryan awkwardly as he realized the Teacher didn't have hands.

Regan nodded beside him. "Go ahead," she said.

The Teacher announced it was finished taking the copy almost before they knew it had begun. Ryan's head was filled with searing pain, yet he didn't want to end the connection in case the Teacher failed to find a way to connect again. It could surely help them. It seemed to know everything. *Seemed to know everything!*

"Wait!" shouted Ryan. "Don't go! Do you know what happened to our parents?"

The Teacher had been a moment away from leaving their minds. Only the pleading and the urgency in the boy's voice could have halted its departure for even an instant. It made a decision and searched key parts of Ryan's memory in less than a millionth of a second, knowing it risked causing brain damage in the young boy. Instantly the Teacher knew the risk had been worth it! It fully understood the significance of Ryan's memories immediately, even though he did not.

"You have to go to your mother now! You only have two hours, so there is no time to waste. She'll die from being hit by that generator if you don't hurry up and stop it."

The Teacher calculated that it was rapidly nearing the point at which the risk of damage to the children was becoming too great and it would be forced to end the connection no matter what.

"I don't understand?" said Ryan in confusion, his head feeling like a swollen balloon about to burst. "Are you saying you know how she disappeared, and where?"

"She didn't disappear," corrected the Teacher, *"you—"*

And with that, their connection with the Teacher ended abruptly.

CHAPTER 22

The Answer

"No!" screamed Ryan, an act that caused additional daggers of pain to plunge into his head. "You *can't* go now! What did you mean?" he demanded.

There was no answer. The Teacher had been forced to leave and would not re-connect soon—maybe never.

While Ryan was just able to withstand the searing pain inside his head, Regan was not. She fell to the ground, gripping her head in agony. Luckily, the immense pain lessened with each second they were no longer connected telepathically to the Teacher. Ryan knew the Teacher had done the right thing. They couldn't take it in their minds any longer, but the timing couldn't have been worse.

Now what? It had told Ryan that they could somehow save his mother but they would have to hurry. But where was she? The Teacher had seemed to know and must have assumed that they did also.

The blinding pain in Regan's head had lessened considerably and was now equal to just an ordinary splitting headache. "Did you hear that, Ryan," she whispered. "Mom's still alive!"

"But she won't be for long if what the Teacher said is true," said Ryan. "And it said that we could do something to save her. But where is she? Where are the other scientists? And how can we save her if *they* can't?"

"Are you sure it wasn't malfunctioning?" said Regan. "It wasn't making any sense there at the end. It said that mom *didn't* disappear. We know that that's wrong."

"Things aren't always what they seem in this place," said Ryan. "Let's assume that everything the Teacher said makes perfect sense—if only we could understand it. And if that's true, then Mom will die in a few hours if we don't figure out what the Teacher was trying to tell us."

"Then we'd better get started."

Ryan nodded. "Okay," he said. "Let's suppose the group *didn't* disappear from the room. Then why didn't we see them?"

"Invisible?" offered Regan.

"Maybe. But I think that counts as disappearing. So let's assume that they were still in the room and easy to see."

"Then how could we possibly have missed them?"

"That's the question, isn't it," said Ryan. His mind

raced through the possibilities. He had to think! Their mother's life was at stake. "The only way is if *we* weren't in the room," he said finally.

"But how can that be?" said Regan. She paused in thought. "Unless there were two identical rooms in the building and we somehow came back to the wrong one. I guess it's possible. That would explain why we didn't see any trace of equipment or people."

"I don't think that's it. Anything is possible in this city, but I'm sure we came back to the same room. And this wouldn't explain why the entrance to the city was missing."

"The Teacher said that Mom will die from being hit by that generator if we don't hurry up and stop it," said Regan. "The Teacher used those exact words."

Ryan nodded. *Hearing* things telepathically made them easier to remember.

"So what does **it** refer too?" said Regan. "She'll die from being hit by the generator if we don't stop **it**. Stop what? Stop her bleeding?"

Ryan shook his head. "No. You would think **it** would have to refer to the generator. This is the only way the sentence would make any sense. But that would mean the Teacher really *was* malfunctioning, because of course we can't stop Mom from being hit by the generator. That has already happ—"

Ryan stopped in mid-sentence. The only way the Teacher's words made any sense was if it *had not* already happened. If it was *going to happen,* but had not happened yet. But if that was the case then . . .

"We traveled in time!" whispered Ryan, his eyes wide.

"What?"

"That's it! I'm sure of it," continued Ryan. "We traveled in time. Why not? We went through a doorway and found ourselves on another planet, why couldn't we have gone through a doorway to another *time*?"

"Like the one we went through when we were leaving the soccer-ball shaped building," said Regan excitedly. "Remember how those three doorways suddenly appeared when you knocked into that podium thing and we went through the middle one."

Ryan's heart raced. What was she talking about? He remembered there being three doorways when he had expected only one, but he had no idea they had appeared suddenly from nowhere after he hit the podium. He must have been too busy recovering from the impact to see this happen. But that would explain a lot. "The podium must have been some kind of control panel. I must have accidentally hit the controls to open a time doorway. When we ran through it, we traveled back in time. To a time just *before* Dad broke into the city."

"That would explain why the entrance was gone!"

"Right. And also why the scientists and equipment and nano-robots were gone when we got back to the room. The Teacher said that Mom didn't disappear, and

I bet I know what it was about to say but didn't [___]
It was, 'Your mom didn't disappear—*you* did'. Nothing happened to *them*. Something happened to *us*. *We* disappeared—back in time."

"So we can still stop the accident from happening!"

"Exactly. And the Teacher said we only had a few hours. So we've almost caught up to the time when this whole thing began. In two hours, the generator will fall on her." He paused. "We traveled back in time a little over a day. When we first checked for the entrance to the city and it wasn't there, we left. I'm guessing if we had just waited an hour or so we would have been there when Dad first broke in."

"That would have freaked him out for sure," quipped Regan.

Ryan laughed. "Can you imagine. He succeeds in breaking through an unbreakable force-field he's battled for almost six weeks, and when he walks through, surprise, *he find his kids already inside*. At that point, if we just innocently said, 'Hi Dad, welcome to the alien city', I'll bet he would have passed out."

Regan grinned at the picture her brother had painted. "This situation really is incredible," she said. "This means there are *two* versions of each of us right now. Our younger selves are probably talking in the woods right now, discussing plans to investigate Proact."

"Very, very weird," said Ryan.

"So I guess we do know exactly where to find Mom,"

said Regan. "Back at the building we were in. She must be there now! All we have to do is go there and warn Mom about the generator before it falls. Then she'll be saved!"

Instead of celebrating, Ryan was deep in concentration. "It might be that easy, but let's think it through carefully," he suggested. "Time travel is very tricky. So what happens if we warn the group about the falling generator and explain about the nano-robots so they aren't afraid of them?"

"Ah . . . we save the day?" offered Regan.

"So what effect would that have?" asked Ryan, and then answering his own question said, "I guess it would change *everything* that happened next. The two of us won't be running out of the building like we did before— the other versions of us won't even *be* in the building yet. So the younger me won't run into that podium in just the right way to activate the time doorway . . ."

"So we'll never get sent back to the past," whispered Regan, catching on.

Ryan scratched his head. "So we—the versions that did go back in time—will never have existed."

"But if we never existed," complained Regan, "how did we save the day in the first place?"

"Good question," said Ryan. "This is why Dad says that time travel is impossible, because it leads to impossible situations. For instance, what if you went back

in time and killed your father when he was a boy—
before you were born?"

"Then you would never be born."

"But if you were never born, then how did you kill
your father?" said Ryan. "And if you *didn't* kill him,
then you *would* be born, and then you *could* go back in
time and kill him."

"Did I mention that I still have a headache from being in contact with the Teacher," quipped Regan.

Ryan smiled. "My point is that it gets pretty com-
plicated and there are a lot more questions than answers."

"To say the least."

"But we do exist now," Ryan pointed out. "So what
happens if we change things so that we never did? What
would happen to us?"

"I don't know. I guess we would just vanish."

Ryan frowned. "That's my guess too. I was hoping
you would come to some other conclusion."

"If we vanish, what would happen to our other
selves? Wouldn't they continue on? No matter what
happens to us, our other selves should be okay."

"I agree," said Ryan. "They'll be us exactly as we
were a day or so ago, but once we change things they'll
live a totally different future than we lived. They won't
remember anything we've experienced."

They paused to ponder the implications of the situation they were in. The prospect of vanishing from existence was quite scary, even knowing their earlier selves would be just fine. But both quickly came to the same, inescapable conclusion.

"We don't have a choice, do we?" said Regan softly.

Ryan took a deep breath and shook his head. "No. We don't. Not if we want to save Mom. When we do, our earlier selves won't go back in time and won't become us. There is no way around it." Ryan's expression turned to one of steely resolve. "But it doesn't matter what happens to us."

Regan knew her brother was right. All that mattered was saving their Mom. Yes, their other selves would live a different future, but it would a far *better* future. A future in which their other selves had a mother, alive and well. "We're wasting time, Ryan," she said firmly, her eyes now glowing with a fiery intensity. "Let's go save Mom."

Ryan nodded, his newfound respect for his sister growing even further. "After we save her we should help the Prometheus team as much as we can before we disappear. Hopefully we'll stick around long enough to report everything we've learned about this city."

They started walking in the direction of the building their parents were in. Five minutes later Ryan stopped in his tracks and said, "Wait a minute! I just thought of something. When we find the team, we're going to have to explain ourselves before they'll believe anything we tell them. Just like before, they'll insist on knowing how we got in here."

Regan shrugged her shoulders. "So?"

"So we'll have to tell them—how we got past the fence and lasers, how we solved the passwords, how we tricked Carl, how we got sent back in time—everything. Then, when we save the day and vanish, they'll have plenty of time to make sure we—meaning our earlier selves—never discover the city in the first place. They'll know to look for the younger versions of us outside of the fence. We'll change our past so that our earlier selves are stopped before they even get *close* to the Proact facility. Do we want that to happen?"

Regan frowned. "No we don't. This city is fantastic. Good point, Ryan."

"Yeah, we owe it to ourselves—well, our other selves—to still discover the city. But we have to save Mom."

"I have an idea," said Regan. "What if we go back outside and find our earlier selves and tell them everything we know. Then they can enter the city and save Mom. We'll vanish, but they'll already be in the city."

Ryan thought about this for a moment. "Good thinking," he said.

They reversed direction and began heading back to where they were now confident the entrance would be waiting for them. This was really going to be something, thought Ryan. How would it feel to talk to himself? Would the old him believe the new him?

The old him was in for the surprise of his life. He wondered where *that* Ryan was now. Still planning with Regan? Maybe hanging down from a tree expecting to be caught at any moment by security.

And with that thought he had one of the most startling realizations of his life. He stopped in his tracks, stunned.

"What is it?" prompted Regan.

"It's not going to work," he said with certainty. "We'll never make contact with our other selves and the generator will still fall on Mom."

"What?" said Regan. "Why do you say that?"

"Because it didn't work the last time we tried it," responded Ryan simply.

CHAPTER 23

A Race Against Time

"What in the world are you talking about?" said Regan.

"They were *us*," insisted Ryan. "The kids were *us*."

"What kids?"

"The kids the guards were chasing. The kids who ran out of Prometheus Alpha. The kids who gave me the break I needed when I was about to get caught. They were *us*. It all happened before. Mom got hit by the generator, the nano-robots swarmed, we went back in time, we figured everything out and we tried to tell our earlier selves so they could warn Mom. *Just like we're about to do now*. But it didn't work. Remember when I was hanging in that tree? A guard saw two kids coming out of Prometheus Alpha. Who else could they have been? Our later selves must have been trying to warn us about the generator accident. But they failed. The

THE PROMETHEUS PROJECT: TRAPPED

guards chased them away from us. So we relived their history. Everything happened all over again.

"And we were just about to repeat history for the *third* time," continued Ryan. "But now we can change things. The versions of us that failed the last time have at least given us the clue we need to change our plan this time. This time we won't try to find ourselves before we've entered Prometheus Alpha to warn ourselves about the generator. This time we'll go directly to the building Mom is in. We'll just hide out nearby until we're certain that our other selves are already in the city."

"But if we do that, Ryan, won't the other you be caught by that guard? The guard won't have any reason to run off when you're about to drop from the tree."

"You're right," said Ryan. "You're absolutely right. We still have to create that diversion for our earlier selves."

"Wait a minute," said Regan. "How did we get in the city the very first time this whole crazy time-loop began? The first time there weren't any time-traveling versions of us to create a diversion. You would have been caught by the guard."

"That's a good point, too," said Ryan. "I don't know. I guess we'll never know. All I do know is that we don't have much time. Regan, we need to split up. You go and create a diversion for our other selves outside. Lead the guards on a wild goose chase away from where we entered the grounds." He paused. "I'll go and warn Mom."

Regan nodded her agreement.

Ryan put a hand on his sister's shoulder. "Regan. I sometimes give you a hard time and I've never admitted it before now, but I think you're pretty amazing in a lot of ways. You have more courage and more brains than most kids twice your age. I'm lucky to have you as a sister." With that Ryan gave her a bear hug, surprising her nearly to death.

"Thanks, Ryan. I can't believe you just told me that."

"Well, I knew this was a great time to be completely honest with you."

"Because we've been through so much together?"

Ryan smiled thinly. "Well that . . . and the fact that in a few hours we'll vanish and your other self will never know I said any of this." His expression turned sincere once more. "But I want you to know that I mean every word of it." He paused. "Good luck, Regs," he said.

"You too, Ry," she replied. She turned and began walking toward the entrance to the city.

Ryan was a pretty great brother himself, and she would tell him this one day, but she wanted to be certain when she did that he actually *would* remember it.

Ryan turned in the direction of the building his mother was in and turned all of his concentration to the task in front of him. He was starving, his throat was parched from lack of water, and his brain still hurt from the connection with the Teacher. But none of that mattered. All that mattered was saving his mom!

But as he walked on he began to become alarmed. Nothing looked familiar. Was he going in the right direction? Thirty minutes later his stomach was tied in knots and he was forced to admit the terrible truth to himself.

He was lost. Totally and hopelessly lost.

It couldn't be! After everything that had happened, after everything they had been through, it just wasn't fair! He should have paid more attention to where he was going as he searched through the city.

He began to run in panic, searching frantically for something he recognized. But still there was nothing.

And he was running out of time.

In just a little while history would repeat itself. Carl, the head of security, would lead the other Ryan and Regan to their parents. They would learn about the Prometheus Project. And then they would try to convince Dr. Harris to let them be part of the team.

And finally, his other self would be forced to watch what he had watched; a generator coming loose from a pole and plunging down to fatally injure his mother.

"Nooooo!" he screamed in frustration at the top of his lungs to the uncaring city. He had better find his bearings, he thought, and he had better find them soon. If not, he would surely fail to save his mother's life—again.

CHAPTER 24

History Repeats Itself

"This is truly a horrible situation with no easy answers," said Carl. "This does not involve criminals, spies from other nations, saboteurs or terrorists. That would be easy. No, this involves innocent kids who are the children of two of our key scientists. Not to mention that Ben here just made an incalculable contribution to this project. Yet the importance of keeping this project absolutely secret could not be greater."

"We won't tell anyone," insisted Regan. "We swear." In the corner of her eye she saw Ryan nod in agreement beside her.

During the last hour they had breached a razor-wire fence, solved passwords, tricked guards and found the greatest secret in the world. It had been the most exhilarating hour of her life. But now that Carl was deciding what to do about this security breach, exhilaration had quickly become nervousness. Her mom gave her a reassuring look but Regan sensed she was equally nervous.

Carl had been thinking silently for some time. "Although I believe it is a great risk, " he said at last, "it may very well be that trusting you to keep this absolutely secret is the best option we have."

Regan brightened. Had she heard right? She had feared *far* worse than this.

"But kids are terrible at keeping secrets—even if their intentions are good," said a plump woman with glasses.

Stay out of this, thought Regan crossly.

"We don't have a choice," said Carl. "Not a real one, anyway." He sighed and turned toward the two siblings, his expression deadly serious. "Listen very closely," he said. "I need for you to understand just what is at stake here."

Regan listened carefully as Carl laid out just how important this particular secret was. She gulped hard. There could be devastating consequences if they failed to keep the secret.

But they would not fail—of that she was sure.

Minutes later it was all settled. Everything had worked out.

But how could you *know* about something this fantastic, this important, without wanting to be a part of it? Without *having* to be a part of it. She knew the chances of Dr. Harris letting them help were near zero, but she had to try. She was willing to beg if she had to. She opened her mouth to speak only to find that her brother had beaten her to the punch.

"Now that this is settled," stammered her brother, "can we . . . well, can we help you explore the city?"

Dr. Harris shook his head. "What? Are you *kidding*?"

"Ah . . . no," said Ryan. "Why not? It's a huge city and you have a very small team. We would stay out of your way and I know that we could help."

Good going Ryan, thought Regan. "Ryan's right," she said quickly. "We *could* help. You could think of us as assistants. We could do whatever you told us to do."

"We promise not to cause any trouble," insisted Ryan.

The discussion continued. Some of the scientists actually thought it was a good idea. Perhaps they had a chance!

She held her breath as Dr. Harris said, "I've already acknowledged that these kids are very impress—"

"Mom, move!" came a frantic shriek from across the room, interrupting Dr. Harris.

Amanda Resnick looked up in shock. It was Ryan! Sweating and gasping for breath. She recognized her son instantly. But Ryan was standing in front of her. How could that be?

"Look up Mom! Please!" pleaded this new Ryan Resnick from across the room, breaking into tears. This show of raw emotion was the only thing that could have broken her out of her stunned daze. She had never seen her son so upset. Something was terribly, urgently, important to her boy. Finally, instead of pondering how there could be two Ryans she focused on what he was saying.

She looked up. A heavy generator that had been bolted to a pole above her was just popping free as a faulty bolt slipped completely from its threads.

She froze in horror as she realized the deadly weight was now hurtling directly toward her head.

CHAPTER 25

Seeing Double

Amanda Resnick dove to the side—crashing into a scientist sitting a few feet away from her on the wispy stairs as the generator-meteor whizzed by her head so closely that it brushed her hair on the way down. She had broken out of her temporary paralysis just in the nick of time. Her husband rushed to her side and helped her to her feet.

Her heart was pounding furiously in her chest. The generator could have killed her!

"What's this all about?" demanded Dr. Harris. "Who *are* you?" he asked the Ryan who had just entered the room.

Ryan ignored him. He ran to his mom and hugged her as tears cascaded down his cheeks. He wouldn't let go. He shuddered as an image of his mom, unconscious, a huge gash in her head, popped into his head. Seeing the generator fall had given him a graphic reminder of what had happened originally—what he had almost been too late to prevent from happening again. She was safe! He was not going to lose her after all.

He had almost given up hope of finding the building. He had run as fast as he could for what seemed like forever searching for his bearings. He ignored his thirst and the searing pain in his head and the burning of his overworked lungs. His panic had grown by the second. If his mom died because he had gotten lost he would not be able to bear it.

And then he had found it! At last! The soccer-ball shaped structure!

But he would have to hurry! Far off in the distance he could just make out four tiny figures entering the building—Ryan, Regan, Carl and Dan. He began sprinting as fast as he could. After running for so long already he now had a knifing pain in his side to match the one in his head, but he refused to let this slow him.

And he had made it! By less than a second.

The adults were too stunned to react as the stranger continued to hug Amanda Resnick, but the other Ryan wasn't. *"Get away from my mom!"* he growled.

The Ryan hugging his mother turned quickly to face himself. Their eyes met. "Don't worry, ah . . . Ryan," said Ryan, feeling silly to be addressing himself. "I'm *you*."

The room was completely silent. Everyone held their breath as they watched two mirror-image boys stare at each other. No one could take their eyes away. The boys were even dressed identically. The only difference in the two was that the newcomer was sweaty and grimy, and looked as though he had slept in his clothes.

"I accidentally went through a doorway that sent me back through time," said Ryan to his earlier self. "So did Regan. She's not here because she had to distract the guards while you were hanging from the tree branch. Otherwise you would have been caught by that guard coming toward you, the one with the walkie-talkie."

Ryan and Regan gasped. This Ryan must be telling the truth! How else would he have known what had happened while Ryan was hanging from the tree. Ryan would have been caught but the guard had to run off to help chase a girl who had emerged from Prometheus Alpha. This really was another version of Ryan. He really *had* already lived through what they were now living. There was now no question about it.

"Impossible," said Mr. Resnick reflexively, but even as he said it he reconsidered. How many other things that were impossible by human standards had they seen already? And what other explanation was there for the appearance of his son's identical twin?

"If you really are my son," said Mr. Resnick, "then you would know . . ."

"Dad, I don't have time for that right now," he said, turning away from the other Ryan to face his father and the other scientists. "I don't know how much time

I have, so I can't play games to prove what I say. You'll have to decide later if you want to believe me or not. I've already changed things so I'll never exist, and I think I'll probably disappear any minute, so I'm going to be quick."

The scientists looked on in fascination, hanging on his every word.

"In the past that I lived through, the generator *did* fall on Mom's head, and it almost killed her. But just when you were preparing to take her to the hospital, a swarm of what we thought were killer insects came up through the floor. They'll be here any second," he added. "We ran and stumbled across a doorway that sent us back in time. We thought everyone else had disappeared, but it turned out that *we* had. We traveled back to just before you had broken into the city, so the entrance wasn't there yet. We thought we were trapped and have been exploring the city for over a day now, searching for a way out. We finally figured out we had traveled in time just a few hours ago."

"How in the world were you able to figure *that* out?" asked his mom in amazement.

"There isn't time for that," he said, wondering how it would feel to vanish out of existence. "I need to tell you the things we've been able to learn. The swarm of insects you're about to see aren't really insects, they're nano-robots. This entire city was built from a single one of these in the same way humans arise from a single cell.

Each of them have the programming to build this entire city. We thought they were the city's immune system at first, but they aren't. After they finished building the city they became its repair crew. They're coming to repair the stairway after you cut a piece out. You're in no danger from them."

As if on cue, millions of the nano-robots poured from the floor, surrounding them. The scientists could not have been more astonished. This boy was telling the truth. Everything that was happening had *already* happened to him. He *had* traveled in time.

They watched in fascination as what still looked like a terrifying swarm of insects devoured rocks in seconds. Even after Ryan had told them they weren't in danger, it was still unnerving.

"The rocks are raw material to be used in rebuilding the step," explained Ryan.

The scientists ignored the insects and focused once again on this amazing boy. He had said he didn't have much time and now they believed him completely. He continued to talk as the insects went about their instant repairs. "The city was built by a people called the Qwervy as an outpost to keep tabs on promising species. They return every hundred years or so to check up on things. The city is set up like a web page on the Internet. Just as you can jump to other web pages by clicking on hypertext, you can jump to other planets just by walking through a doorway. The Qwervy don't go web surfing, they go *planet* surfing. But Earth is off limits until we become more mature."

The scientists listened in fascination. How had these kids possibly learned all of this in a day? They each had dozens of questions to ask but no one dared interrupt.

As Ryan had spoken the insects—nano-robots—had completed their work and disappeared without a trace. They had repaired the stairway just as this new Ryan had said they would.

Ryan was about to tell them about the zoo and the visit to the wooded planet when he realized that he hadn't told them about the most important thing of all; the computerized, telepathic Teacher. If they could find the Teacher they could get answers to all of their questions. "There is a schoo—"

Ryan stopped in mid-word. *The scientists had all frozen in place!* Like living statues. As if time had stopped.

And Ryan had a sinking feeling that this could only mean he was vanishing from existence and that this collection of living statues would be the last thing he would ever see.

CHAPTER 26

The Challenge of Prometheus

J ust then Ryan felt the Teacher's presence in his mind once again and he somehow knew that it was also in contact with Regan, wherever she was. The Teacher had succeeded! It had learned how to connect with them again. Ryan was not in the process of vanishing from existence, after all! At least not yet. What a relief!

"Children, please listen carefully. The world appears in slow-motion to you now but it is not. Instead, you are in fast-motion. I have speeded up both of your minds because we have far less than a second. When you saved your mom and changed the future of the Ryan and Regan in this room, and thus your past, I was able to complete key time calculations. The precise instant the timeline will un-kink and you will vanish is nearly upon us.

"But I can not and will not let this happen. At least

not before I have taken some critical steps to ensure your safety. That is why I have contacted you now.

"I do not take these steps lightly, but you two are quite worthy of them. I fully expected that you would be after coming to know you from the copies of your minds, but the insight, selflessness, bravery, and heroism you have shown since we parted has left no doubt. You both possess the qualities of will, mind, and decency that are needed by your species, and the adventure you have taken together since passing through the time doorway has further enhanced these qualities and enriched you both. These qualities are more than worthy of preservation.

"For this reason, in the instant before the timeline un-kinks, I will transfer all of your thoughts, memories and experiences to the Ryan and Regan in this room—even the memory of the words I am now speaking. Your bodies will vanish as the new timeline dictates they must, but only after you have been transferred to new bodies—your own. Bodies you are familiar with in every way.

"Brace yourselves, children, it will happen . . . now."

The experience was indescribable. There was a flash of light a thousand times brighter than the brightest summer day, yet it didn't cause them any discomfort. In fact it was glorious. Then, suddenly, they were accelerating to near infinite speed and experienced every thought and every memory they had ever had all at once. It was exhilarating beyond belief and . . .

Slam! With a mighty jolt, the transfer was complete.

The scientists came back to life, moving normally again.

Regan, who had been hiding from the guards in the woods outside, now found herself back in the large room inside the soccer-ball shaped building. She was staring at her brother—but only for an instant! Before she could even blink he vanished without a trace! Ryan, standing beside her, also saw his mirror image disappear the instant the transfer had been completed.

Every scientist in the room gasped at the same time. The boy who had barged in on them and saved Amanda Resnick's life had been right again! He had vanished as if he had never been—just as he had predicted. The other Regan must have also vanished from wherever she had been. Everyone looked over to Ryan to reassure themselves that at least *one* of the Ryans remained.

One Ryan did remain. And that Ryan felt *fantastic*. The searing pain in his head and side were gone. His hunger and thirst were gone.

This was terrific!

Suddenly the room stopped once more. Everyone turned to living statues as they had before. This time the kids knew what this meant: the Teacher had returned.

"Hello children. I have accelerated your minds again because we need to have a private conversation before you speak with the others. Because of this acceleration,

you are now thinking so quickly you won't have time to form words, so remember to 'think' your words—don't try to speak. How do you feel?"

"Fantastic," thought Ryan.

"I have scanned your minds and I am happy to report that the transfer was a complete success."

"Thanks. Thanks for everything," both kids thought in slightly different ways. Without the Teacher they would never have saved their mother—or themselves.

"You are very welcome. I have truly enjoyed getting to know you. But, unfortunately, this will be the last time I will establish a connection with you."

"Why?" thought both kids in disappointment within an instant of each other.

"I have been in contact with the Qwervy. Humans were not supposed to find this place for hundreds of years. The Qwervy have the power to remove this city from your planet and erase all human memory of it. But they have chosen not to. Instead, they have decided to let you proceed so they can learn how your species will handle this opportunity; how you will explore, what you will learn, and how you will apply this knowledge.

"But all of your actions must be your own, without my help. What you learn you must learn for yourselves. The Qwervy believe your species has great potential, but also a dark and destructive side. The Qwervy doubt you are ready for what this city offers, but by naming this project Prometheus you have shown surprising in-

sight into your own nature. This has given the Qwervy reason for hope. You are a primitive people who have been given fire—now what will you do? Will you use it to heat and light your grass huts or will you use it to burn down the grass huts of your enemies? Or perhaps your entire world?

"I will be watching, but I cannot interfere. My greatest hope is that your species will prove able to play with this fire responsibly. Your species will need to face, and pass, the challenge of Prometheus. If you do, you will have taken a giant step closer to gaining entry into galactic civilization."

Ryan and Regan were silent, digesting what they had been told. Was humanity ready for this responsibility? They would soon find out. There was no turning back now.

They both understood what the Qwervy were doing and why, but they had grown fond of the Teacher in a very short time. *"So we can never speak with you again? About anything?"* thought Regan sadly.

"This is probably so," answered the Teacher gently. *"But then again, never is an awfully long time."* The Teacher paused. *"I have to go now, children. But before I do, I need you to promise that you will not tell the others about me."*

"We promise," they both replied earnestly.

"Thank you. Please understand that this means that they cannot know that you two are the Ryan and Regan

who traveled in time, nor about the transfer I made possible. You will have to pretend that you know nothing about how the time traveling Ryan and Regan were able to learn what they did."

"We understand," they replied.

"Good," thought the Teacher. *"I realize you have already been asked to keep this city a secret. I hate to burden you with even more secrets, but I know you are up to the task."* The Teacher paused. *"Well, I'm afraid it is time. Goodbye children, and good luck. It has indeed been an honor."*

Ryan and Regan thanked the Teacher warmly once again for all its help. It was hard for them to imagine how things could have turned out much better.

"Can I just ask my brother one quick question before you go," asked Regan.

"Certainly."

"Thanks," she thought happily. She turned her attention to her brother who had no idea what was coming. *"Ryan,"* she began innocently. *"Did you really say that I have more courage and more brains than most kids twice my age? Am I remembering that right?"* she teased. *"Yeah. I'm pretty sure that's what I heard,"* she continued, laughing in her mind.

Ryan groaned. *"Just my luck,"* he complained. *"I say something nice about you one time and it comes back to haunt me. We were supposed to vanish so you wouldn't remember that."* He pretended to be horrified but his thoughts were filled with obvious mirth.

"I can still arrange for you to vanish if you would like," offered the Teacher playfully.

"Ah, that's okay," Ryan quickly replied. *"No need to go to that trouble."* He paused. *"I guess I'm stuck with what I said then. I guess I'm never going to be able to live this down,"* he finished lightheartedly.

"I don't know, Ryan," came his sister's equally lighthearted reply. *"As a very wise Teacher once said, never is an awfully long time, Ryan. Never is an awfully long time."*

CHAPTER 27

Part of the Team

Dr. Harry Harris walked over to the spot from which Ryan had vanished and examined it with raised eyebrows. Only his memory and the still startled and awestruck looks on the faces around the room told him this had not been a dream.

He shook his head in wonder. "Amazing! Simply amazing! How in the world did these kids learn so much in such a short period of time? And the heroic way that Ryan saved your life, Amanda. Outstanding. And who knows what would have happened in our panic if we hadn't been warned about the nano-robots. I almost had a heart-attack even *after* being warned."

Dr. Harris turned toward the kids with a new respect. "Thank you both. You were wonderful. I realize that now that your mom has been saved you won't ever accidentally activate a time doorway. And because of this, I also realize you will never accomplish what I just thanked you for. In fact, the two of you won't even know *how* you managed to accomplish these things."

Ryan and Regan glanced at each other knowingly and barely managed to suppress a smile. Dr. Harris couldn't possibly imagine that the Ryan and Regan who had accomplished all of these things were still very much in the room.

"But it doesn't matter to me," continued Dr. Harris. "For we have witnessed a demonstration of your enormous potential. We know for certain what you are capable of achieving. We have seen the strength and courage that you both have inside. Clearly, your skills and problem-solving abilities are good for more than just defeating security measures. And just as obviously you are quite capable of handling yourselves in this city, without supervision and in desperate circumstances. Not only did you save the life of a critical member of the team, but the information that Ryan provided us is incredibly valuable. Incredibly valuable. We owe you kids quite a debt of gratitude."

They both beamed as Dr. Harris rubbed his chin in thought and then smiled. "And I think I know just how to repay you?" he continued. He glanced over at their parents questioningly and they quickly returned nods of approval.

"You mean . . ." said Ryan eagerly.

"That's right," said Dr. Harris warmly. The corners

of his mouth turned up in a small but delighted smile. *"Welcome to the team."*

The Resnick siblings were giddy as they surveyed the room full of smiling and encouraging faces.

What an opportunity. They were being offered the chance of a lifetime. *More* than the chance of a lifetime. Who knew what awaited them inside this strange and fabulous city? Who knew what adventures? What dangers?

Snooze-ter Pennsylvania was turning out to be not such a boring place, after all. They might not know just what awaited them in this alien city, but they knew this for sure; it would be interesting. And exciting. And fun.

"Carl," said Dr. Harris. "Can you contact the president for me when you get back outside."

"What should I tell him?"

"Tell him I just recruited two capable new team members for the Prometheus Project," said Dr. Harris.

He smiled broadly. "And tell him that I expect big things out of them."

The Adventure Continues...

The Prometheus Project
Book 2
Captured

A Fantastic Alien City

Ryan and Regan Resnick are the youngest members of a top-secret team exploring the greatest discovery ever made: a vast alien city buried deep underground—as potentially deadly as it is astonishing

A Devastating Invasion

When the city is captured by highly trained soldiers led by a ruthless alien, the adult members of the team are taken hostage. Now, Ryan and Regan are the team's only hope of survival.

A Diabolical Plan

With the future of the world at stake, the Resnick kids must do the impossible: outwit the brilliant alien, free the prisoners, and thwart an unstoppable invasion. But not everything is as it seems. And time is quickly running out. . .

About The Author

DOUGLAS E. RICHARDS is a former biotechnology executive who has written extensively for the award-winning magazine, *National Geographic KIDS*, and also for *American Fencing Magazine*. He currently lives in San Diego, California with his wife, Kelly, his children, Ryan and Regan (for whom the main characters in his Prometheus Project series are named), and his dog Dash. After graduating with a BS in microbiology from the Ohio State University, he earned a master's degree in molecular biology from the University of Wisconsin and a master's in business administration from the University of Chicago. To learn more about Douglas and his work, please visit *www.douglaserichards.com*.

8